The
Preacher's Daughter

Coco M.

Published by Around H.I.M. Publishing
For publishing information, address:

Around His Image Marketing and Publishing
5 West Hargett Street #210
Raleigh, NC 27601
info@aroundHim.com
919-208-5658

For information about special discounts for bulk purchases, please contact the author at cocojm2015@gmail.com
www.cocojm2015.wix.com/author-blog

Manufactured & printed in the United States of America

Unless otherwise identified, Bible quotations in this volume are from the King James Version (KJV) and
The New International Version (NIV) Bible Translations

ISBN-13: 978-1515030768
ISBN-10:1515030768
First Edition

Acknowledgements

This book would not be possible if God had not been first in my life, especially when I didn't even know it. I truly understand now what it means to put Him first in my life. I give Him all the glory, the honor and the praise for working in my life.

I want to acknowledge and relay thanks to my husband, who has really taught me what a real man should be. Thank you so much for supporting me. I love you.

To RNCC, my church family; thank you for listening to my testimonies without judgment. A special thank you to my Pastors Dr. Jeffrey Chapman & First Lady Sandi Chapman for teaching me the Word of God, in a practical and real way so that I am equipped to allow God's Word to lead me and guide me; especially through this Book's journey. I so do appreciate your love and support.

To VOW, I love you.

To my God Sister V and my God Brother -continue to dig your ditch. Love you both.

Thank you to my typist and proofreader, Mrs. Sheila, for your support and assistance with my very first project; love you much.

This Book is especially dedicated to my daughter who has always made me proud. From the time of birth until now, you have become one of the most able and brightest young women I know. Always dear heart, keep God first in your life and everything else will be added unto you.

Table of Contents

.

THE PREACHER'S DAUGHTER

"Start children off on the way they should go,

and even when they are old they will not turn from it."

Proverbs 22:6

"The Ideal Child"

Here's my story, and I hope that in sharing my life and testimonies with you, my reader, that you or someone you know will be delivered and blessed and set free from all the generational curses and spirits that may have come on you throughout your life. You see, whether you know it or not, the people you deal with daily –whether it is a boyfriend or friend – sometimes will have spirits attached to them which can be transferred to you by just being with that person for a long period of time, both as a friend or lover. I'll go into more detail later in the book.

I remember, around the age of 5 years old going to church with my mama, and I have to say, let's be realistic – just because you go to church at such an early age, does not make you a perfect person, even though God is instilled in you at such an early age. And, just because you are a preacher's son or daughter, does not mean you will be the perfect child. In fact, there is an old saying among a lot of people which says *"preachers' kids are the worst ones"*. For the most part, that is not true, but I was one of those kids growing up that people would say was one of them.

Mocking mama, I heard my father say in his usual drunken state. "I'm going to church again". My mama's reply was "yes and you *should* go too instead of always drinking". "Get on outta here woman and go on to that old crazy church with all those crazy folks." He said. Sitting always near the front of the church, in my mama's arms at revival was the usual thing for my mama and me. I remember vividly when the usher rushed over to us and said something in my mama's ear and from the look on her face, I knew at that age it wasn't a good thing that was told to her. I would watch my mama's face a lot to see if she was in a good mood or not; yes, even at that age. We immediately left church, and when we pulled up to our building, I saw the most fascinating thing I had ever seen so far in my young years and that was a big red truck in front of our tiny duplex apartment with flashing lights and lots of police cars. When we saw my father, he was sitting on the ground crying and my mama asked "What happened?" "I forgot the pot of collards was on the stove" he said, still crying. We had to go and stay with my grandmama until they got our place back in living condition. When we moved back into the apartment, this time we had neighbors beside us. I was glad we had them because it was my aunt, although her stomach was much bigger than it was the last time I saw her. My aunt hugged me and said "Not before too long you'll have a cousin to play with." I remember being so happy because there were not a lot of kids to play with where we lived; just old people, so I grew up with what they call an *old soul*, simply because I could carry a conversation with most people at a very early age and I knew a lot of things at my age that most kids didn't know.

A couple of nights later, there was a loud knock at our door; it was my auntie. I could hear my mama crying so I got up out of my bed to see what was wrong. When I entered into the other room in our apartment, all I saw was blood on my auntie's shirt and her face. I had never seen anything like this before. I went to her and said "I love you –why do you have red stuff all over your face and shirt auntie? She said "Baby, it's okay; your uncle's been drinking again and got a little upset with me, so I came over here and now I'm okay." So I went on back to bed, but this happened quite often --the loud knocks and all -- but not the red stuff.

I remember the exact day my baby cousin came home from the hospital because it was the same day that more flashing lights came to our building, but they were the blue flashing lights this time but I still knew that something was wrong --just by association from the last time. As we stood on the porch, these men approached us, with some papers in their hands. I heard them ask if we knew this person who had the same name as my uncle. Just about that time my uncle came out of his door with tears in his eyes and said "That's me." They then told him he was under arrest for suspicion of armed robbery. A few days ago my uncle was in the car when some people he knew robbed the bank –to take the weight of financial stress off my auntie. As he was led away, he looked at my auntie and said "I love you and I'm so sorry." This was devastating for my family, especially for my father because this was his drinking buddy.

The next time the lights came I was outside playing with my dog having loads of fun –just the two of us. All of a sudden, I stopped and I ran into our apartment and grabbed my daddy's leg and said "Daddy, don't go." He said "Baby, what are you talking about?" I said to him "The blue lights are here again." We both walked to the door together but this time they were at one of the other neighbor's apartment. I was so happy; I went back to playing as if nothing bad was going to happen. These turn of events must have had some strange effect on my father because guess what, he had begun to go to church with us. He didn't go every time with us when we went, but at least he was going to that crazy church with all those crazy people.

The next time we attended church it was very different. This time people were crying and were sad so I was sad too. There was this big old square thing at the front of the church with lots of flowers around it. When it was our turn to go and look in at it, I saw my granddaddy in it asleep. Then, after a short while, we left the church and sent to this place with all these stones sitting on the grass. People were still crying and the preacher was preaching again, but this time it was outside. My mama kissed me and held me tight and said "Your granddaddy will always love you. He just has to go away for a little while." See, I figured that since they had closed the box, put it down in this deep, deep hole and covered it with a lot of dirt, that I wouldn't see him for a while because I knew it was going to take a long time for him to dig his way out; little did I know it would be the last time I would see him also.

"And how can anyone preach unless they are sent? As it is written: "How beautiful are the feet of those who bring good news!" Romans 10:15

"My Daddy's Call"

At the tender age of 10 years old, I remember packing up my clothes to move into our new home –yes, a house. *This was the most beautiful full house I've ever seen in the world*, I said to myself. We were finally moved in and I loved my new room. I had all white furniture just like in a doll house. By this time, church was a usual thing for all of us. My daddy really enjoyed going to church. One night in our house, I remember seeing him crying as he was sitting next to me while I was saying my prayers. I asked him what was wrong and he said "Nothing baby. God is just speaking to me." He then tucked me in and kissed me goodnight. I noticed that my daddy would cry more and more. I was worried about him. Then, one day my mama said "Come here baby, I want to talk to you." She sat me down between them both and said "Guess what baby girl; you are going to have a new playmate." I said "WOW, auntie is having another cousin baby for me to play with?" My mama replied "No dear, you're gonna have a baby brother or baby sister to play with all by yourself." So, as the months went by, my mama's stomach began to get fat just like my aunt's did.

One evening I remember putting on a special dress for church. My mama was dressed up too, and I noticed that my daddy had a special suit on. When we got to the church my daddy was missing. I asked my mama where he was and she pointed to the place where the preachers all sit together. I saw my daddy sitting up there (on the pulpit) with his head down. Then a man stood up and said this is my son; I am so pleased and honored to be presiding tonight because I've watched this young man grow in this church, and tonight, he will bring forth the Word of God.

John 3:3-7 "Jesus replied, "Very truly I tell you, no one can see the kingdom of God unless they are born again." "How can someone be born when they are old?" Nicodemus asked. "Surely they cannot enter a second time into their mother's womb to be born!" Jesus answered, "Very truly I tell you, no one can enter the kingdom of God unless they are born of water and the Spirit. Flesh gives birth to flesh, but the Spirit gives birth to spirit. You should not be surprised at my saying, 'You must be born again.'

My daddy's first sermon was entitled "There Must be a Change". I was so happy I cried happy tears right along with my mama because my daddy was now a preacher, however, little did I know the attacks of the enemy was getting ready to take place in my life, as well as my parents' lives. First, the women came from everywhere. There was this one particular incident I remember very well. One night, my daddy was not at home and my mama rushed to put me in the car, then she waddled to get inside herself, still pregnant. We pulled up to a hotel and drove around to the parking lot until we came to a stop. I looked around and there was my daddy's car, so I figured we must be meeting him there. My mama told me to "Lie down and wait right here, inside the car." Waddling, she walked out of my view so I peeped over the seat; you know how kids are. A few minutes later she came back to the car to get me. As we walked up the stairs I noticed my mama began to cry. We got to one of the doors of this hotel and she knocked. It took a few minutes but when the door opened, there was my daddy in nothing but a towel. I peeped around him and there was this woman there too. She was in the bed. My mama slapped my daddy and then went after the woman. All I saw was a lamp, a towel, soap, whatever flying across the room. Finally the woman made it to the door screaming with nothing but covers on her. My daddy was saying "I'm sorry! I'm sorry! It's not what you think. Stop throwing stuff". I was laughing and crying all at the same time and guess what -- I was looking for something to throw myself. We went straight to my grandmama's house and spent the night there.

The next day my daddy came to talk to my mama, and the next day, and the next day, until finally one day mama said we were going back to the house. I was so happy because I missed my room. Then my daddy came home later that same evening from work, full of tears, with his head hanging down which was something he had never done, except for the time at the hotel. When he finally came home, he was the man I used to see when I was very little; yes, he was drunk, very drunk; so drunk that my uncle had to bring him home. My uncle started explaining to my mama how my daddy got to where he was so that he could bring him home. Then, all of a sudden, my mama grabbed her stomach as if she was hit directly in the stomach or something like that. I had never seen my daddy straighten himself up so quick after being drunk. He immediately rushed my mama to the hospital and my uncle took me to my grandma's house. Sometime later I heard the phone ring. I heard my grandmama say "Breached! Oh my God and they are gonna operate on her now?" I knew my mama was the only one within the family who was in the hospital, so I started to cry, thinking that I would be seeing my mama in this square box thing –just like my granddaddy, with flowers all over it. That's what happened to granddaddy. He was in the hospital for surgery and never came back.

After grandma had finished talking on the phone, she picked me up and sat me on her lap and began to say "Baby, we're going to the hospital." I started crying even more and told her that I didn't want to go, and she asked why, so I told her

"I don't like going to the hospital because the hospital is a bad place. Every time somebody goes there, they never come back." She began to explain what happened to my granddaddy; she told me that he was really, really sick but that my mama was going to be alright. She continued to tell me "Your granddaddy is in heaven" she said. Well, since I had heard so much about heaven in church, I knew she was telling the truth. When we got to the hospital, there was this baby wrapped up in a blanket with a hat on its head; yep, I had a little baby brother to play with.

"Becoming a Teenager"

By this time my parents were building their second house which meant we had to move again. I thought I would die. I was about to be in junior high school and I had to make new friends all over again. My first day of school was horrible because I was the new kid in school and my parents were well to do by now so my clothes were name brand only because my aunt would send them from New York.

Gloria & Calvin were my jeans. As I looked around at the other girls, I didn't see these name brands except for the white kids, so immediately I had the title of being a stuck up rich black girl. One day I came home crying so for the next day I selected and prepared my clothes to wear for the following day. I tried to find something that had no name. I found a pair of rust colored corduroys. Happily, I said tomorrow shouldn't be so bad; oh how wrong I was.

One morning, as soon as I got on the bus, they all

began to laugh at me, but I dealt with it. When we arrived at school, I hurriedly got off the bus and headed to my locker. When I arrived at my locker, I ran right into the girls' school bully. When I bent down to open my locker, she placed her foot on the door of my locker so I couldn't open it. I stood up and asked her to move her foot; she laughed. As I looked around I could see that she had quite a few followers on her side. I said to her "Oh you're gonna move your foot because I ain't gonna' be late for class. I let her know that I wasn't scared of her. Guess what happened —she moved her foot. From that day forward, we were the best of friends. See, she knew a lot of things about life; things of which I didn't know because most subjects on life and sex were forbidden in my house, unless it was pertaining to church, so she would school me on most things. She would tell me stories about both she and her boyfriend and how they would do stuff, so I wanted to experience some of the things I thought I was missing. These were some of the best years of my life and also some of the worst. She was a good actress and could play the sweet child role very well so my parents would let her spend the night with me and sometimes I would spend the night with her. The only difference with me spending the night with her was that I would always try to do it on the nights when we had our dances at school. I had begun to develop into a shapely young woman and I was always told that I was a pretty girl. It didn't take long for guys to notice me, even more so than they did at school; the only difference now was that I didn't have an excuse for being late for class, which is the excuse I would use to not talk to them.

Now, along comes Sam (*name changed to protect the not so innocent*). I let him tell me what I thought I needed to hear. We would sneak behind the building at dances and I would let him feel on my body. It felt real good to me and it felt real good to my body and I would allow him to kiss me passionately. There would always be this feeling that made me feel good down there, so at the next dance or game, he would talk me into sneaking somewhere with him and we would do the same thing again and again, each time taking it a little further –just like my girlfriend told me to do.

Eventually, we began to skip school and go to his place when his parents weren't home to play around but never fully engaging in the actual sexual act. Each time the feeling would get stronger for me in that area, until one day I let him unzip my pants and place his hand in my forbidden area. It hurt a little at first, but then it began to feel different; not good, just different. See, the enemy knows how to entice you. Sometimes it happens little by little and then sometimes it comes all at once. For me, most of my wrong doings and my behavioral issues happened all at one time because I didn't have a true fear of the Lord. Then we would take it even further, so much so that we began to go to my house – oh, I meant my parents' house.

One day we were sitting on the couch, alone in the house, because my parents didn't get home until about five thirty in the evening so I had a good two hours on my hands every day of the week while they were at work. Looking back now, I should have been doing my homework. Anyway, we were on the couch and he began to do what he did best and that was whispering Satan's sweet words (or pillow talk) of pleasure in my ear and I listened to him and I obeyed. He would say "Come on baby, we've been together for three months now and all we do is feel on each other. Don't you love me like I love you and if you do, then prove it to me and let me have some." I thought to myself *"Oh, his hands feel so good; maybe I'll let him."* But sex to me, at this age, did not feel good the way some people described it would; maybe for the guy it feels good, but for the girl, it's not such a good feeling, at least not for me.

Well, wouldn't you know, we kept skipping school and having sex. He became my first love and lover in a matter of months. I was walking around school thinking I was all *that*, then rumors began to surface that the same lover I had was a player and was notorious for getting girls to go to bed with him. I didn't believe it because most of the time he was with me. There was even a rumor that he had a baby on the way by this girl name Jill. I had seen them walk home together some times but I paid it no mind because his best friend, who was also Jill's cousin, was always with them. Several months went by and I began to notice that Jill's stomach was beginning to grow; ewe, she *was* pregnant. It hadn't even crossed my mind that it could have been his baby she was carrying. Anyway, one day we were at my house, oops, my parents' house lying on my bed. Of course by now you already know what we had been doing. He said I have something to tell you.

He told me that what was being said around school about Jill was true; that he was the baby's daddy, but that they had only done it one time and he went on to say that he didn't love her like he loved me, and that I was pregnant too. "WHAT! Boy, you must be crazy. I ain't pregnant." "Yes you are; I felt the same way with you that I felt when she got pregnant." Then the strangest thing happened; I heard the garage door opened up. *It's only four o'clock; this can't be happening, I thought*, but it was. Sure enough it was my daddy walking in the door. "Oh boy, now what do we do, he asked. "Quick, hide in my closet, I told him." Then when I saw my father, I said "Oh, hi daddy!" "Hi", he said while looking around for something or somebody. "Whose bike is that outside?" I responded "What bike?"

"Girl, I'm gon' give that boy two seconds to get outta my house." Sam took off running through my room, but not before my daddy popped him in the back of his head and dared him to ever come back. You already know what happened to me; see, back then kids didn't know anything or wouldn't dare dial 911.

The next day at school everybody knew what happened and they were having a good laugh from it. I even laughed to keep from crying from embarrassment. Still, I had to address what was said to me, after school I waited for Sam. Guess who he showed up with, yep! Jill and she had the nerve to grab his arm and hold on to him like they were a couple. She looked at me and said I heard what happened and began to laugh. I looked at her and said, *(sarcastically)* "Yeah, well I see what happened to you." She sarcastically replied "Yeah, heard about you too; you'll be walking around like this in a few months." I wanted to pop her dead in her mouth but I listened to elderly women talk and they use to say that a man should never hit a pregnant woman so I figured a woman shouldn't either.

I looked at Sam and told him I needed to talk to him. He told her to wait for him around the corner. I asked him "What's goin' on?" He said "I already told you –you're pregnant." "Stop saying that" I replied. He says "Why? It's true. Wait and see 'cause I know you're gonna have my third child." "Your third child"? "Yeah, my third child." This girl I use to mess with in Kenwood had my son. "I don't see him much but I love him. Jill gon' have a girl and you gon' have a boy too." "Forget all this baby talk" I said. "What about us?" His reply was "You can't even take company; I can spend the night over Jill's house. Her mama loves me." *Now I'm thinking what kind of mom lets her thirteen year old daughter have a boy spend the night.* Then I started thinking *what was wrong with me asking him what's up with us when he is clearly sleeping with both of us.* One plus one was definitely two now, that's when he would see her, at night. "So whatcha saying"? "I'm saying you pregnant" and he walked away laughing.

<u>1 Peter 4:3</u> "For you have spent enough time in the past doing what pagans choose to do—living in debauchery, lust, drunkenness, orgies, carousing and detestable idolatry."

"My Baby's Daddy"

Mrs. May, you may now bring your daughter in. "What are your symptoms, the nurse asked; are you experiencing nausea, vomiting?" "No." I lied. "My stomach just hurts like the flu or something." Now, here comes the question from the doctor… "Have you been sexually active?" Well, you know what the answer was, but before I had a chance to answer the question, my mama answered it for me, and rather quickly. "Of course not"! Then the nurse tells me to "use this cup", so I did. Well, the test came back negative, so I was admitted to the hospital for further testing. Back during those times the tests were not as accurate as they are now. So the outcome of this was to take medication for acid build up in my stomach which was called acid disease; today it's called acid reflux disease. Well, one month went by and I was still sick –regurgitating and passing out, so my mama took me back to my doctor. Again, my doctor asked the question "have you been sexually active"? Again my mama answered for me, but this time with an attitude. "Just figure out what's wrong with my baby, will you!" "Okay. We will have to do some more extensive testing so I'm going to admit her to the hospital again."

I'll never forget the day my doctor walked in my room at the hospital and asked me again, "Have you been sexually active?" I lied, yet again. But there was no way of getting around this one for the blood that runs through your veins can tell a lot about you, and they had taken plenty of it. My mama was devastated. Notice I said mama (and not parents); we couldn't tell my father this had happened. A baby at fourteen years old, and with my father's status in the church –oh no; I couldn't mess up his future or mine. I remember my mama crying and praying all the way to *the other* hospital, and then crying and praying all the way home. We never spoke about the situation again.

Exodus 20:13   "You shall not murder."

You would have thought that I had learned a lesson and that my mama would have finally talked to me about sex but she just said "Don't do it again." Sam was back in my life and yes, I still loved him. By now, I was fifteen and thought I was even more grown than I was at fourteen. Sam just had a way with himself that I couldn't leave alone. Even though I knew I wasn't his only girl, I thought I would still be his best girl. As if I was an expert on sex, eight months later, there I was, pregnant again. This time we had to tell daddy. There was so much commotion in my house that day. I remember my grandmother saying "Boy, you could have killed her!" My father's response was "I don't care about all that. She knows that I'm a bishop in the church and if this gets out, she knows and we all know how people will talk."

My grandmother said "Grow up. You think she's the only one that has gotten pregnant in the church. It's plenty of them that have --you just don't know about them". My daddy went on to say "…and no one will know about her 'cause she ain't having it. She done had one already –they hid it from me", my daddy said. My grandmother was in shock so this time my aunt stood up and said "Well, ya'll should've talked to her about sex then instead of avoiding the subject. She needs to know about these things; she's not a child anymore. This could have been avoided. You should have put her on something." "Oh no", my mother argued. That just gives her a go ahead to do it more." "If you hadn't kept her so locked up all the time she probably wouldn't have even gone through this at all, my aunt continues. You have to talk about these things with your child so that they don't get fooled by people and let them learn about life instead of their friends influencing them, like becoming sexually active." So that was two babies gone.

Exodus 20:13 "You shall not murder."
Please, always remember this scripture.

Of course I was banned from ever seeing Sam, my two babies' daddy, ever again and I was told, or shall I say demanded to not have sex again, with no one. But still, I was not given any education on the subject. This didn't stop me. It just made me want to see Sam more. According to the letter I left that my nosy little brother found in my room, I even ran away; he went in to wake my dad up to read it. I think I had gotten half way down the street when I heard my daddy calling my name. Ten minutes later, I am jumping over chairs, trying to hide in corners of the room from my daddy's belt, and of course, with my nosy little brother laughing on the other side of the room. I wanted to strangle him for getting me in trouble – and so soon just after my *attempted* run away departure.

So I started skipping school again, specifically, to go over to Sam's house. Thankfully, I had an aunt who I could talk to about anything, so she took me to get some birth control pills. In the meantime, we got engaged and snuck around when we could. It's crazy how you can always find a way to do the things you're not supposed to do. The next time I was able to go anywhere alone that my parents knew about was when I was sixteen and it was a football game; I went only because I had to twirl my flag in the band. Now unofficially engaged, I got the most devastating blow. My boyfriend/fiancé' had two babies now by Jill. She had gotten pregnant again over the summer. See, I didn't tell ya'll that Sam was a year younger than I was, so when I went to high school, Sam and Jill were still in junior high school. I didn't get to see him as often because I was in high school, but when I did get to see him, he couldn't deny them babies. They looked just like him. Young and dumb me, still skipping school to be with him, almost cost me to be left behind a year in school that year. I had missed so many days in school (well past the limit you were allowed) that my band and chorus teacher, who was very influential at the school, had to talk to the principal for me to pass my grade. Young love was not what I thought it was. So here was yet another "I told you so" chapter in my life.

Comment: Remember that old idiom…
'Fool me once, shame on you; fool me twice, shame on me."

"Mr. Melody"

Remember Lay's Potato Chips catchy slogan: "Betcha can't eat just one" or the saying that goes 'once you start, you can't stop', well there is also a belief that when you've been with someone sexually, you pick up the spirits (be them good or bad) of that person and the people they've been with? So now, I began to have sex anywhere I could, whenever the time would permit: during church revivals, I would be in the back seat of my parents' car. Of course I was supposed to be in church listening to the preacher, but no, I was outside fogging up the windows of my parents' car, and you know what, I would go right back inside at the appropriate time just like nothing had happened. Scared? No, I wasn't scared, but you have to admit that I was very bold to even think about fornicating on holy ground.

I met this new boy in church who I had a crush on. He played the organ so well which made me excited just by striking a few chords. And, well, I had a voice to go with the organ too so there was an instant attraction between us. All of the girls wanted Mr. Melody, but they weren't bold enough to get him nor could they dress or sing like me. I would only see him once a year but that once a year thing was good enough for me. I was bragging to my friends that I had taken his virginity. We ran up phone bills and wrote letters to each other until our parents realized that we were too serious about each other. I even drove to see him on the sneak –two hours away. I told my mother I had to work all day (I now had a job) and he told his parents that David, one of the guys he played for sometimes, was picking him up. Away we went to David's house and sinned for about four hours. I didn't see him until that next year and every year thereafter during our annual church rally. Our interest and attraction toward each other was the same but much more intense each time. I couldn't wait to see him –not just for the sex but because I truly believed this man was my soul mate.

His parents were bigwigs in our church and because they lived out of town, they would spend the weekends of the annual conferences with us at our house. Anyway, we would sneak into the den when everyone was asleep and have sex, grinning at each other the next day at church like it was nothing. I had even introduced my friend at church to his brother and they began to do the same thing. We would be in the den, all four of us with no shame and no fear or reverence for God or our parents. Stupid! How stupid we were! Every day he was in town we had sex. He was hooked and so was I; every year for three years we did this. We said we were engaged and planned on being together for a very long time, like maybe even get married one day.

It was time for me to go off to college and he was still in high school. Yeah, I can imagine what you are thinking –another young guy right… exactly, four years younger than me. I taught that boy some things he'll never forget. When our parents found out, I was whipped, he was whipped. I actually fell in love with this guy and I knew he loved me too. After all, you never really get over your first love, right? Rest assured, you will hear more about Mr.

Melody in book two.

"Fresh Meat"

That's what they (the men) call you when you're a freshman in college. Wild child is all I can say; yep, that's what I was. Not having to answer to anyone but my teachers was great, or so I thought. Pretty soon I wouldn't even be answering to them either. Smoking became an everyday thing now that I was of legal age and could also buy alcohol too. Well, it didn't take long for me and my roommate to find the weed man. See, we went to high school together and had already talked and decided to be college roommates. On my way to the café for dinner, my girlfriends and I (yes we were high, which was most of the time by now), met this chocolate man who was the prettiest man I had ever seen. He dressed so preppie. We were standing in line waiting to get our tray (he already had his tray), and I caught his eye on me and I tried to play it off but he smiled and I smiled back. A few minutes later, my girlfriends and I found our seats and as fate would have it, and little did I know that we were always seated in the same area he was. You know how you can feel someone watching you, and you turn around and sure enough, they were? Well, he smiled at me again and motioned for me to come over. First mistake right there; I should have let him come to me. In hindsight, it really wouldn't have made a difference. Anyway, we began talking to each other, saying "I've been watching you for a long time now and I like your style. You're not like most of the other freshman around here, huh?" You see, he was an upperclassman, so he knew I was young and dumb; see, what he was doing was pumping my head up.

This man had me crazy for him. He knew all the right things to say at first and get this – he wasn't rushing me to have sex. He would say "Baby, when you're ready we'll go there." I finally told him that I was in love with him and he said the words right back at me, and, well, that was all she wrote. Later on that evening, I snuck in his dorm room, because during that time they didn't have co-ed dorms. Actually, I was taking the risk of getting thrown out of school and so was he, but I guess we both didn't care; all I knew was that I had waited long enough to really feel what

I felt through his pants when he would kiss me. "Whew! was all I could say. The sex was out of this world. This man made such sweet love to me I would do anything for him – and I do mean anything.

Often he would send me back to my room with a swollen belly and pains that would bend you over if you laughed too hard. I would go to his room the next day and days after that. I would always end up going back, addicted to this man's lovin' as well as him. Too good to be true, huh? Yeah, I know; there is always someone else when you are in college, like another lover in the picture. You might ask "Well didn't you see the signs; didn't I see this coming?" But I say no; this man was smart. He had met my parents and likewise, I had met his parents. I saw no signs of this man cheating on me. We were together all of the time, except for when he would go home for our breaks from school. When Homecoming came around, I had noticed that he started becoming distant from me. I attributed this to his frat brothers. He said he was going home for the weekend and would not be attending the Homecoming game. I was okay with this and made plans with my girlfriends. We were leaving the game and going down the hill to our dorm to make us some more drinks for our cups and I saw what looked like the back of his head going to his dorm building which was right after mine. I did a double take and pointed him out to one of my friends, just to get her to confirm what I thought I saw. My man (or so I thought) was holding hands with someone, so I take off running and so did my friends. We caught up with him and I then tapped him on his shoulder. He turned around and you could have sold him for a penny. I asked "what's up" and he responded with same, "what's up" back. I introduced myself, not as the girlfriend, but as a friend of his. She did the same, however she introduced herself as *the girlfriend*. I had my thinking cap on; I was very smart. I got all the information I needed, from her, by telling her "he talks about you all of the time, so where do you live"? She replies "I'm from (get this people, same place he's from), and she continues saying that she is attending school in DC (which was actually twenty minutes from where we were attending school). She asks, "So which dorm do you live in?" She proceeds to share that she has a friend there and that maybe the next time she comes to visit she will stop by to say hello. I reply "cool" and gave her a hug; gave him a big hug with a kiss on the cheek and told them to have fun.

About two hours or so later I was paged to come downstairs. I looked out the window and saw his car so I told one of my girls to tell him I am not here. This made me feel like I was in control of the situation, however, the only thing I was not in control of was the *suicidal thoughts that were flooding my head; how, when and where I was going to do it.* I had planned to use pills because with pills no pain was involved. I told my friend I was going for a walk to clear my head. By this time I was good and drunk. I put the bottle of pills (Aspirin) in my pocket and headed out the door. Well, I didn't know my friends had seen me place the pills in my pocket, so they followed me to see where I was going and then they went straight to his room to get him.

I had gone to the football field, because from there, I

could see his room and, if the light was on, I knew he would be there. I was so upset, I'm cursing, drinking, pacing back and forth and crying my eyes out, all the while, telling myself just how hurt and stupid I was. Well, a short while later, I look up and guess who is running towards me; yep! It's the cheater himself. He grabs me and shakes me so hard I threw up all over his shoes, and mine. He begins to console and comfort me. "Girl, what are you doing? Your friends said you were going to try to kill yourself." Then he asked me was it all over between us because of what I had seen and been told today. I replied "What do you think?" He began to explain that she was not actually his girlfriend –that I was and that he was only entertaining her because she came unexpectedly to Homecoming with both his parents and her parents and that he did not want her to feel embarrassed because she hadn't told her parents they had broken up yet. See, they were supposed to get married after college and she didn't want them to know yet because it would hurt them. Then, he continued on saying "Don't you know how much I love you. I would never do that to you."

Well, after a few hours had passed by, I got real bold and spent the night with him, even though I knew college security would probably do a room search, but I didn't care; I needed to be with him, specifically that night to see if she would come back or call. Well she didn't so I believed him. This man was sticking to me like white on rice for months. After several months had gone by, and before he went to class one Friday, he stopped by to tell me he was going home for the weekend. Immediately my mind went into reverse mode about the girl; I knew he had a late class so I had my girlfriend take me to this girl's dorm, which again, was twenty minutes away. It just so turns out that she was there, in her room, packing too. She remembered me and started spilling her guts to me about how he proposed to her, when the wedding date was, how long they've been together (which was since high school), and finally what time he was picking her up, because you see, they were getting a hotel room to celebrate their fifth year anniversary of going steady.

We both waited for him to get there, so when he

knocked, I offered to get the door for her so I could surprise him. When he *sees me*, the look on his face was as if he had lost his bottom jaw, which is what would have happened if I had slapped him like I wanted to, because that's how low it was hanging. I wanted to hurt him now as well as her, so I told her who I really was and how long we had been involved with each other. I continued to tell her how I had been to his parents' house and how he had been to meet my parents, what his room looked like, what his private looked like (which was hooked to the left, I might add). I told her everything I could think of so that she would be totally convinced of what I was saying was the truth. She was definitely hurting just as bad as I was, so my mission was accomplished. After a few minutes, I looked at him and walked out the door. Can you believe he had the nerve to try to explain his self again! This time I was smart and I didn't take him back, but I figured I would use him for a sex run every now and then, or as they call it today, friends with benefits. "What --you say!" They do it to us ladies, don't they?)

If I could begin my life anew – to start my life fresh, I would change the part of me which couldn't wait to have sex for fear that I wouldn't fit in. Also, smoking weed and cigarettes, drinking -- all are spirits that are hard to get rid of to this very day. I promised myself that I would be a mother who would always be available for my child to have a conversation with me about anything and everything, if I was ever given that chance again. Don't get me wrong, I'm not taking anything away from my mother, but I wished I had that bond with her that I so desperately needed at that time of my life. I not only disrespected my parents, but the most important thing is that I betrayed God and cursed my life, my parents' lives and my children's lives every time I did it.

Exodus 20:4-6   "You shall not make for yourself an image in the form of anything in heaven above or on the earth beneath or in the waters below. You shall not bow down to them or worship them; for I, the LORD your God, am a jealous God, punishing the children for the sin of the parents to the third and fourth generation of those who hate me, but showing love to a thousand generations of those who love me and keep my commandments."

Exodus 20:12 "Honor your father and your mother, so that you may live long in the land the LORD your God is giving you.

1 Corinthians 6:12-20 "I have the right to do anything," you say—but not everything is beneficial. "I have the right to do anything"—but I will not be mastered by anything. You say, "Food for the stomach and the stomach for food, and God will destroy them both." The body, however, is not meant for sexual immorality but for the Lord, and the Lord for the body. By his power God raised the Lord from the dead, and he will raise us also. Do you not know that your bodies are members of Christ himself? Shall I then take the members of Christ and unite them with a prostitute? Never! Do you not know that he who unites himself with a prostitute is one with her in body? For it is said, "The two will become one flesh." But whoever is united with the Lord is one with him in spirit.

Flee from sexual immorality. All other sins a person commits are outside the body, but whoever sins sexually, sins against their own body. Do you not know that your bodies are temples of the Holy Spirit, who is in you, whom you have received from God? You are not your own; you were bought at a price. Therefore honor God with your bodies."

All soul ties come with every one of the person's soul ties, so you just don't sleep with them. You sleep with every person they have been with. You can't add that up.

"There are physical, mental, emotional and spiritual aspects of sexual intercourse. There is often significant emotional trauma associated with sexual immorality and it usually manifests itself in a variety of ways, including the development of a soul tie. Soul ties are exactly what they sound like. They are ties from one person's soul to another person's soul. According to 1 Thessalonians 5:23, this scripture refers to man, made up of three parts: spirit,

soul and body. Soul ties are intimate bonds to another human being."

(Adebayo, Debbie "Soul Ties- The Emotional Trauma Associated with Sexual Immorality" www.singlepleasingthelord.com . 1/26/15. Internet)

"Mr. Smiley"

The prettiest teeth I ever did see on a man. His name for the purpose of this book will be called Smiley. He was this sweaty, running, shortest shorts wearing brother I had ever seen. He was on the track team and I had to be the one infatuated with him. You would have thought I had learned my lesson with chocolate men, but oh no, this running man I had to conquer. He was walking into the café with his track buddy whom my roommate had a crush on and the teeth were showing as usual; I've never seen anyone running and smiling, both at the same time.

I knew I was a fine catch so to pull him was easy. By this time I had learned a few tricks from the guys, so I walked up to him and introduced myself. He smiled and told me his name and I asked him what his major was and told him mine and from there we hit it off. We started seeing each other just about every day; see he didn't live on campus which was most impressive to me. I would get picked up from my dorm and I would take him to work and pick him up from work in his Ltd. I didn't mind that because it was the biggest car I had ever driven. Anyway, he would always bring me a sandwich from his job where I picked him up from every night.

See, he lived with his drunken uncle, a crazy aunt, an obese cousin and a weed-head cousin, who I got along with very well, I might add. Watching his drunken uncle was just like watching a movie whenever his cousin and I were high. See, we would sit for hours sometimes and trip off of him stumbling in the yard and cursing out his wife. Then there was his female cousin, who I didn't trust at all. The reason why is because I knew this girl in high school who use to baby sit for her sometimes. She always had the backseat of her car loaded with kids. You know, as a woman, we have this female intuition somewhere in the back of our brain, so I called one day and the cousin was rude, as usual, but this time she gave up some information. "Look, she said, "you are the fool; he is just playing you. He goes with the girl across the street." Well, I couldn't wait for him to pick me up for the weekend. We would get a hotel or motel room at least twice a month. He could afford it because he was working and I was well worth it. I was in love with this man, but not as stupid in love as I was before. I was calm when he picked me up and yes, I did confront him. He didn't lie. He replied "Yeah, we use to be tight, but now it's just that I feel sorry for her; her parents have somewhat disowned her because she got pregnant." So I said with a hint of excitement "Pregnant! Is it yours?"

He replied "Hell no." So I said "Tell me. How do you know it's not your baby?" He replies "'Cause ever since I met you I haven't messed with her; can't you tell how much I love you." Yeah, right, I chuckled to myself. *(When have I heard that before and how many times have I heard it!)* From that moment on it was on. I learned how to please a man at an early age and I also promised myself that I would never be hurt like this, in this manner again. He would be like silly putty in my hands when I was finished with him.

I was out for blood! So, in the park, the back seat of his car, the football field, the counter at his job, his bedroom at his uncle's house, any hotel, any motel, anywhere we could do it, we did it. Oh yeah! He was sprung and by this time I had learned *ALL* the tricks of the trade. See, I had a friend that showed me how not only to drink out of a coke bottle, but also how to *really* use a coke bottle, thereby using the bottle to please a man. I started dressing sexier and I changed my hair style to wearing braids. I started wearing a little more makeup and last but not least, not always being available for him when he paged me; I was a definite turn on for him as well as for myself.

This man (Mr. Smiley) was a dog and I knew it, but then, so was I. This chocolate man was a regular on my list and so was the other guy I had dated every year (Mr. Melody) of whom I saw once a year during our annual church convention. He was now attending school twenty minutes away from me. I thought we had a good thing going for a while, but then twenty minutes away eventually became a problem; we were getting real serious so I had to start ducking him. See, he was about to blow my cover, because he missed my chocolate man one day by about five minutes 'cause he was paging me from downstairs. I told you I had learned quite a bit already, even though I was still quite young.

Smiley had another friend who ran track with him from Tennessee. I noticed Smiley would come with him on a regular basis when he came to pick me up. I had to know why so I made myself as friendly to him as I could without my crossing the line. Well, wouldn't you know it; we will call the name of his friend Tennessee. Tennessee was the one who actually crossed the line. He told me he had fallen in love with me and then he told me began to spill his guts about how many there were, what dorms they lived in, how he would drop me off and how he would visit each one and then tell the whole track team his stories the next day.

Pretending that it didn't bother me, I went about my business as usual, but every time I would see Smiley something was different. Different than anyone of these other men I had been involved with. *I knew, even though there were other girls he was involved with, I knew Smiley loved me.* This became even more apparent as we were about to break for the summer. He kept telling me how he would miss me and how he would come to see me on the weekends since it wasn't that far for him to come; deep down inside, I wanted to see him too.

Well, he kept his promise. Over the summer my parents bought me a car because I was doing so well in school; *yeah, right.* I would hide my grades when they came in the mail and yes, the academic probation letters too. I wasn't even considered a student anymore to myself. I was doing my own thing. Wake up smoking weed, go to bed smoking weed, go to class when I felt like it or just to show my face, which was mostly on test days, thinking I could pass them anyway. All hell broke loose when I drove up to his uncle's house in my new car. The high school chick did have her baby by now and was back on the hunt. I rang the doorbell and she answered the door, smacked her lips and called his name. He came outside, kissed and hugged me like we hadn't seen each other all summer long. You already know how my demeanor was. "What is she doing here?" I asked. "Baby, come on now; you know what she does for my cousin; this is not my house and I can't tell her not to come over here." "Prove to me you love me", I said, "let's move in together". *What! Am I crazy?* "I can't believe you just said that; that's exactly what was going through my mind" he replied. Then, the biggest shock of all was when he replied, "Yes, let's do it!". *Oh no! What have I just done? I thought to myself, how do I get out of this?* "I was just kidding baby. I know you love me" I said. Then he says "So what are you saying? You saying you don't love me enough to live with me?" "No, I'm just saying I know you help your uncle out around here and besides, how will we afford to pay rent to someone; I don't have a job." Alas! That did it! *Girl, you good*! I was thinking to myself. But then his reply knocked me for a loop. "Baby, you know I can get a second job. I'm not taking that many courses this semester. By the time you get back in a few weeks, I'll have everything done." *Okay, I can do this and still maintain my playgirl status; yeah, I can do this*, I thought to myself all the way on the drive back home.

Then, guess what else just popped in my thoughts... *How will I get around this with the Reverend and First Lady —my parents?)* Daddy was quite popular in the church. Mama, well she was always a diva to me; she was the heart and soul of my daddy, so she wouldn't be that difficult. By this time we had started to have those girl talks, so she already knew what time it was (so to speak).

Sorry, I got off course a little bit. Anyway, how do I tell them? I'm thinking to myself, *to act normal when I walk in the house and take a deep breath and just tell them.* But, that day never came. I went back to school as normal but I did take a detour to our new one bedroom apartment. Not the dorm that my parents were paying for. The day would soon come when I had to tell my parents that I had moved off campus with my roommate from school, without their permission. But I didn't tell them it was a man. My daddy was furious about the idea but my mama soothed him and said "she's doing so well in school and she's really matured a lot honey". I think this will be good for her and it will teach her responsibility. Though he still didn't like it she had won him over; what's done is done.

As time went by my mom calls and says "We're coming to see you this weekend." "Aww mom, we who?" This was a very important question I asked her. "Why your father and me silly." "Um, mom, I have something to tell you." "What, you and that boy are living together?" and then she laughed. I said "Ma, how'd you know?" "Mamas know child." So then I ask her "Does daddy know?" "Girl no; I'll leave that to you and your friend to tell your father." My heart sank in the pit of my stomach. I told Smiley and he said "Well, I love you and you love me, so what's wrong with that?" I tell him, "Are you brain dead or something? What's wrong?" What's wrong?" "You know my father's view on shacking up; you've heard him say it for yourself."

That's what it's called by old school people – shacking up, but now it's called living together, however, the Bible calls it for what it really is – and that's *sin*. By mid-morning there was a knock on the door, so I took a deep breath and opened it. "Hey daddy", I said and kissed him on the cheek. He was his usual affectionate self and mama always gave me big hugs and kisses. Daddy and mom look around the apartment, so I ask "Well daddy, do you like the apartment?" He looked over his glasses and said "No, you are supposed to be living on campus." "Daddy, I am a junior now; it's okay. "Uh uh," he said. Another knock came on the door and guess who it was; yep, Smiley. Come on now; y'all know I'm a smart cookie by now. "Hi Smiley" I said and hugged him. (Smiley and I had decided that we would pretend he did not live with me and that he would occasionally stop by to say hello.) He says hi to everybody, hugs my mom and shook my daddy's hand then we all sat down for lunch. Let me tell you --I can really cook because my mama taught me how at an early age.

<u>1 Corinthians 7:9</u> "But if they cannot control themselves, they should marry, for it is better to marry than to burn with passion."

<u>Hebrews 13:4</u> "Marriage should be honored by all, and the marriage bed kept pure, for God will judge the adulterer and all the sexually immoral."

<u>1 Corinthians 7:2</u> "But since sexual immorality is occurring, each man should have sexual relations with his own wife, and each woman with her own husband."

<u>1 Thessalonians 5:21-23</u> "...but test them all; hold on to what is good, reject every kind of evil. May God himself, the God of peace, sanctify you through and through. May your whole spirit, soul and body be kept blameless at the coming of our Lord Jesus Christ."

<u>Genesis 2:24</u> "That is why a man leaves his father and mother and is united to his wife, and they become one flesh."

<u>Romans 12:2</u> "Do not conform to the pattern of this world, but be transformed by the renewing of your mind. Then you will be able to test and approve what God's will is—his good, pleasing and perfect will."

So how are you doing in school?" "Fine", I lied, because since Smiley and I had been living together I was tired most of the time and I would not get up to go to class —not even for a test. I had basically quit and got a little part-time job. What can I say -- I like having money!

"Uh huh", my father was talking directly to Smiley now "So how long you been living here son?" I almost choked on the food that was in my mouth. My mama didn't flinch. "Sir, I love your daughter and she loves me and one day we're gonna get married." "Married"! I never heard those words before. See, even though we were living together I still had this notion that he was still cheating because he would come home late sometimes, saying that he had stopped by his uncle's house.

By this time I was quite the detective. I had already timed, from the time he got off of work to the time it would take him to get over there and I had already called, so I did one of my daddy's numbers "uh huh". Smiley never knew I knew though. Anyway, my father says one day to Smiley "You're supposed to be married before you defile my daughter and her bed." They went on and on, back and forth and my daddy finally said "I will not come back to visit with you anymore until you're both married, and son, you're not welcomed in my house anymore until you do the right thing by my daughter."

I was in tears for days; once again I had disappointed my father. My mama said "Don't you worry about your daddy; he'll come around." So I continued cooking, cleaning, fornicating every night and working. Though we weren't married, it sure felt like it. I had gone to the grocery store one day after work to get a few groceries; I was unloading the groceries onto the counter and waiting for the total. All of a sudden I felt hot; I began to see little white spots in front of me and I broke out into a sweat. When I finally opened my eyes, I was behind the cash register with people standing over me asking was I okay. They called the rescue squad and told me not to move. The rescue squad arrived and took me to the hospital. In the process of fainting, I had somehow hit my head. Smiley was called and he immediately arrived to the hospital shortly after I did. They took blood work, examined my head, took X-rays, and finally the doctor came back in with the results. "Your head looks okay, but guess what —we found that you're pregnant." I fainted again.

When I came to, I was still in shock, and I am now thinking to myself, *what am I to do now*? That's all I could say to myself and Smiley. I was already out of school without my parents knowing it and now I have to decide what to do with this baby (my third pregnancy). Of course Smiley was happy about it and immediately said "Let's get married." "No" was my reply. *I can't marry you* (I was thinking to myself) being that I knew I couldn't trust him. Then it hit me; this man really does love me in spite of his infidelity. I have to tell my parents or I could just do the usual; have an abortion.

But then something stirred in my soul. No, keep this one. This one is meant to be. I waited and waited until it was about my eighth week of pregnancy. Okay, now I'm thinking to myself *"It's time to tell your parents."* I took a deep breath and called my mama. The phone rang and rang on the other end and she finally picked up. "Hey mama." "What's wrong", she asked. "Oh nothing; I was just calling to see how you guys are doing." "Baby, what's wrong" she asks again. "There's something I have to tell you", then I began to cry. "Uh, I'm pregnant." "Baby, why? Not again!" She began to cry along with me. "How could you not have been on anything and you know what has happened to you in the past." "I *was* on something Mama; it just didn't work I guess." "You're not gonna keep it are you?" "Mama, aren't you tired of this sin --of killing children? You are supposed to be a Christian." There was a long silence over the phone.

Then, the next statement that came out of my mama's mouth was something that killed me inside that very day. "You cannot bring that child home. You will embarrass me and your daddy. If you don't kill it, I will disinherit you. You and that child are not welcomed in my home" and just like that, she hung up the phone. I called my grandma – which was her mama, and told her what she said. She was crying harder than I was and immediately called my mama on a three-way conference call. I had never heard my grandma say a bad or curse word, until then. These were words I didn't even know she knew that were coming out of her mouth. When she finished, my mama was repenting to God, to my grandma, to me, the neighbors, the dog, and anybody else who might have been listening.

"That's your child!" That was the last thing I remember her saying before she hung up on both of us. It was a few weeks before I spoke to my mama again. I figured I would let her call me. When she finally did call, it was as if she had never said those awful things to me like she did the last time we had spoken. So I acted like I didn't remember those words either. Nevertheless, it still hurt. "So, what are ya'll gonna do?" "Mama, we've been talking about marriage, but I'm just not ready mama." "Why not", she asked. "Because I think he cheats on me." "Girl, please; every man is gonna have their days of cheating." "Yeah, but I don't have to put up with that." Well baby, there are some men who are dedicated to their other half. Uh huh, anyway, you just deal with that when and if the time comes, but for right now you think about marrying that boy. He's a good man and he loves you to death."

Both Smiley and I talked about it some more when he got home and decided to go ahead and make that move for our new unborn child. I called my mama the next day and told her and of course, she was so happy and started planning right away. I would wear my prom dress and they would buy his suit. My cousin would be my bridesmaid and his drunken-state uncle would be his best man (oh my goodness – what were we thinking). Of course we couldn't invite that many people; only family because I was showing a little and we couldn't risk my daddy's reputation by letting anyone know that his little girl was pregnant without being married first.

The wedding went well and my pictures came out like prom pictures, except they were on instant camera paper (that's Polaroid, for you very young folks). Of course this "special day" was not my true dream wedding of how I had expected my wedding to be, but if we had more time to plan, it would have been much more elegant; what was done was done and after the ceremony was complete I was ready to leave. Morning, noon, evening and night sicknesses had already set in several weeks before our wedding. I was sick so bad that on the way home we had to pull over for me to regurgitate –twice, just from smelling his uncle's alcohol from the back seat of the car.

"The Honeymoon"

We pulled up at our new apartment, opened the door and walked in. Still feeling a bit sick, I went into the bathroom to get dressed to put on my little teddy to prepare for our lovely honeymoon night like I had seen on TV but my belly just wouldn't let me function like a new wife should. So I told my husband that I didn't feel well and the night wouldn't be like we'd planned. The next thing I knew I was being dragged to the bed by my hair and I heard him say "Oh, it will be like *I* planned; all you have to do is lie there". So I did. I remember thinking to myself *what just happened? Is this the way a honeymoon is supposed to be? It was certainly not like the one I had seen on TV.* I called his mother and told her what happened and she said "Oh no baby. He promised he would never do that to a woman because his daddy used to do that to me every day." When I handed him the phone I could only hear one part of the conversation – his, saying "yeah, yeah, yeah" again and again, then "no", and then he hung up. He apologized to me teary eyed and we went to sleep. For the next four months I was really sick and then one day I went to the bathroom and ended up on the toilet in extreme pain. I called him at work and by the time he made it home I was bleeding real heavy. We finally made it to the hospital and as I sat on the table I remember thinking about the baby that was growing inside of my belly and saying to myself and to God, *please let everything be alright.* See by now I had begun to feel the little flutters they had told me about throughout my doctor visits. The doctor came in and asked me what was happening? I told him about my day and what I had felt on the toilet and he asked me to lie down on the table. I did and he began his examination. "Well Mrs. Smiley, it appears that you've just had a miscarriage, but to be really sure, we need to get some blood and look at the levels. I'll have the nurse come in and then I'll check back with you when the lab results get here; I'm so sorry." What! I lost the baby; it seemed as if my whole world had just come tumbling down. I really wanted this baby; it was the only thing I knew I could count on right now.

The past four months, with my husband, had been hell to deal with. Although he had apologized to me on our honeymoon night, it didn't change a thing. He still continued to be abusive physically; never hitting me with his hand, but pulling my hair, choking me but in a way not to have bruises. So somewhere in the back of my mind I blamed him for the miscarriage because it was a stressful situation. I was already too many miles from my parents to visit them on a regular basis, and forget about calling and telling them what was going on; huh, talk about don't ask, don't tell. That's what I was taught. Sometimes a man will get angry with you so it's best to just do what he asked you to do so you don't have confusion. It's called being submissive my grandmother use to say.

Keep the house clean, cook his food and do your wifely duties in the bedroom, no matter what. Anyway, the doctor came back in and said "Mrs. Smiley, what we suspected is true. We need to see you back in this office in six weeks. When these things happen, remember that there was something that was abnormal about the pregnancy and the body responded this way to make sure you have a normal baby. After you come in on your next visit, we will talk about your conceiving again. In the meantime no activity until then, ok?" I called my mama and told her what happened and she cried. I heard her tell my father on the other end what had happened. He said "Hum, huh, oh, she can try again", just like that --with no feelings whatsoever. I remember asking myself *does this man have any feelings at all?*

The trip home was more than quiet. So many thoughts raced through my head; thoughts of anger, hurt, resentment, regret, and happiness. Happiness you ask? Yeah, happy that now maybe I could get a job and get away from him sometimes, just to have some peace. I had it all planned out. I would work at night. In that way, I wouldn't have to see him at all, plus we only had one car. We didn't talk much the next two weeks. It's as if he knew that I blamed him so he left me alone. Then out of the blue (while getting ready for bed that night) sky he asked "the roll my eyes in the back of my head question". *"How long before we can do something?*" I said "The doctor said we have to wait until my next visit with him." "I don't think so." He said. I replied "But he said I needed to wait so I wouldn't risk getting pregnant in my tubes." "Girl, I got condoms; get in this bedroom" (but I tried to get out). Later on, when I woke up, I was lying naked on the bed, still slightly bleeding with a big knot on my forehead, probably from one of his many head bunts, no doubt.

That was my last draw. I made up in my mind that the next week would be my job hunting day. Just me and my two best friends (left foot and right foot). I never had a problem finding a job; I could work anywhere and any place, and right now all I needed was to get a check. I could save up to get my own place. I knew I didn't want to go back home to hear a constant... *"I told you so; if you'd done what you had to do while you were in school you wouldn't have to go through this. Look at you already divorced --and in the first year. In this family we make our marriages work. What am I gonna tell my congregation"?* So I knew I had to make my own way. Well, the following day was unsuccessful and so was my night --like many of my nights. Weeks went by, which seemed like months, with no phone calls and the usual we'll call you for an interview, after reviewing my application, if necessary.

After a few weeks had passed, it was time to go back for my six weeks' checkup. The doctor began his ultrasound. He paused and said hold on a minute, after which he called the nurse over. She looked puzzled, just as much as he did. "Mrs. Smiley, guess what –your tubes are okay and so is your baby." "What! What! Just what are you saying doctor" I yelled and he says to me to please calm down; it's going to be ok. So I immediately asked him "But how?" He replied, "I don't know. In your physical exam it appeared to have been a miscarriage, and in addition, your blood levels had dropped quite a bit." The nurse looked at the doctor and said maybe twins; he said, yeah, it had to be. I knew I had still been feeling those flutters but they were much stronger now.

So, here I am now, almost four months pregnant and

didn't even know it. My husband was so happy he began to cry, and the doctor asked him was he ok; he replied, "Yeah doc; this is probably the happiest day of my life. I love my wife so much and we still have our baby." I looked at this man in disgust with a smile on my face thinking, *you sneaky man; it was your fault I thought that I almost lost this baby in the first place. How dare you sit here and portray to this man that you are the perfect husband. I should burst your little bubble, but I knew if I did what was going to happen when we got home and I couldn't take that chance, because after all, I had a baby inside. I couldn't wait to get home to call our parents. Hey mama, guess what; I'm pregnant still."* Huh! How? I thought you had to go to the doctor today to get clearance? Yeah, I did but when they were looking at the ultrasound, they saw the baby and said it must have been twins.

"Oh baby, I'm so happy for you. Hold on. Rev, pick up the phone." I heard the other receiver pick up and overheard mama say "She's still pregnant; it was twins, then my father says "Thank God you didn't have two babies girl;

how in the world would ya'll have taken care of two babies on his income." "Hang up the phone dummy" my mama said. "Don't worry about him. Wait until the baby is born; you won't be able to stop him from calling to see how the little one is doing. Do you know if the baby is a boy or a girl yet?" I told my mother that we didn't want to know; we just want a healthy baby. We talked about how they made a mistake for a few more minutes and then hung up, but not after saying our usual "I love you" to each other. My mama always had my back even though I felt she didn't. Sitting there thinking about the conversation I had with her, I went back to the part where I had told her we just want a healthy baby. What did I just say —we, no, I really meant I because there is no we. I am looking for a job and my own place.

A few days later, I returned to job hunting. I remember it being very hot one particular day when I was walking back to the apartment. Once in the apartment, I sat down just to cool myself off. I ended up falling asleep though; when I woke up guess who was standing over me yelling "you ain't cooked nothing yet"? What have you been doing' all day girl. So I replied, "I was tired boy, now move" and if you can't wait for me to cook then do it yourself. I went into the kitchen and took out the fish sticks and fries and slammed them on the counter. Then I proceeded to walk pass him, then I immediately felt a jerk in the back of my head that landed me on the floor so hard that it seemed like the floor shook right under me.

The pain that I felt in the bottom of my belly was so strong that I had no other choice but to scream. He looked down at me and said "Oh baby, I'm sorry"; he picked me up and took me to the bedroom. Then he says "I'll run you a hot bath." I was lying there in pain so long that the bath water he ran was cold by the time I thought about it again. I went in to use the bathroom and when I was done, I saw blood again; more blood than before. I yelled so loud that Ms. Fletcher, the old lady from upstairs knocked on the door and asked if I was alright. She was always knocking on the door asking if I was alright; I think she heard us fussing all the time so she knew what was up.

I rushed to get dressed and ran to the car. Mr. Smiley, driving what seemed to be the slowest speed ever to me, saying over and over again "I'm sorry, I'm sorry". Yeah, I know was what I was saying every time those words came from his mouth. We finally arrived at the hospital emergency room and they rushed me into a room and asked what happened. "Yeah", he answered before I could get it out and said "well she fell down the steps at our apartment", then cut his eyes at me as if to say you better not say anything different either.

The doctor went ahead and performed another ultrasound and internal examination and said "well everything looks okay but we want to keep you overnight to make sure that your placenta is still intact". I was okay with that -- just to get a break from Mr. Sorry was a good thing. I rested well that night and I thought about everything that had happened so I had decided to chalk it up and call my parents to come and move me out. However, to do that meant I would have to tell them everything that had been going on.

Just as I picked up the phone to call my mama the doctor walked in. He said "We need to do another internal examination. Your blood test came back slightly low. It could be several things happening so we need to check you out thoroughly again. I'll be back with the nurse." A few minutes later they were back. He did the examination and said to me "Mrs. Smiley, your cervix is dilated two centimeters. Have you had anything that feels like cramps in your vaginal area?" "Yeah", I said, "all night". "We're gonna have to give you some medicine. I think you are having contractions and at four months the fetus would not survive." "Fetus, you mean the baby don't you?" "Well, it's just a term we use." "Well my term is baby and I would appreciate it if you use that term with me." "Okay" he said. "I know this has been a difficult pregnancy for you and you're frustrated but we're gonna do everything we can to save this baby. You'll have to stay in the bed for a couple of more days and we'll check again to see how you are doing." Dummy was sitting there the whole time with tears in his eyes. I wanted to thump him in both of them. *"This is all your fault,"* I thought to myself. I laid there and thought, *how dare you even think about shedding one tear.*

As I continued to lie there in bed, I thought to myself *"Get it together girl, the doctor said you had to relax and not stress."* I knew that the continued stress on me would make the baby stress in the womb so I decided not to call my parents, yet; anyway, he had been there day and night being nosy, as if he really cared. I think he was just worried that I would tell the doctor what really happened. Two more days had passed and I couldn't take it anymore so I told the nurse I was gonna take a shower today; no more sponge baths because they just weren't getting the job done. The nurse made me sign this paper saying they wouldn't be responsible for me getting up out of the bed because the doctor's orders said complete bed rest.

I signed the papers and took a quick shower every day for the next two days. It was time for the doctor to do another exam; the nurse came in and when the doctor was done this time, he said "We need to get you to ultrasound ASAP". "What's wrong" I asked? "I just need the radiologist to confirm something for me because I can't get a heartbeat." "No heartbeat; what does that mean?" "Just let us get this test done and I'll be back in Mrs. Smiley." I began to pray; *"Father, I stretch my hands to thee, no other help I know. If thou withdraw thyself from me where ever shall I go? God, I know that you are a God of mercy and you're full of grace and I need your grace right now. Touch my womb and heal this baby that has been conceived in sin. I offer this child back into your arms as a living sacrifice holy and acceptable unto you. Bless this baby with a good loving spirit for your kingdom building. Let this baby not stray from your word. I speak life to the lungs, heart, limbs and every fiber of the baby's body and I call this baby a servant of yours now and forever; nevertheless thy will be done. I ask this in your Son, Jesus' name, Amen."*

When we arrived in the Ultrasound Room the radiologist immediately said "Weight looks ok; measurement is ok" and then there was a long pause. "There it is –heartbeat is ok." "Thank you Jesus, thank you Jesus" is all I could say and I heard His response to me "anytime my child, anytime". That was as clear as I had ever heard it. Sometimes it would scare me when I heard His voice. I used to think I was crazy until a prophet told me what it was. One Sunday this prophet looked straight at me and called me up to the altar and said *"God has given you a great gift; don't misuse it. You will hear His voice clearer and see things too. You also have the gift of healing in your hands; stop running. I have called you to be a leader and not a follower. You will be a fisherman for my kingdom. Yokes will be broken when you open your mouth and call sin for what it is, sin. Healing will take place; souls will be saved through your worship in song. You are the strong one, God said."*

Well now by this time I am back in my hospital room waiting for the doctor. My husband looked at me and said "Aren't we the luckiest parents." I looked at him and rolled my eyes and said "You mean blessed, don't you?" *Dummy,* I thought, *"don't you even know that there is no such thing as luck; everything we have, everything we do, everything we get is all because of God."* Anyway, the doctor came in and said, "Well I have good news and I have bad news; which do you want first?" I replied "The bad news first because I already know the good news." He said "the bad news is that you can't go home right now because despite our efforts to stop you from dilating, you're dilated to four centimeters now and you are barely passed your twenty weeks. At this point, if you were to go into labor, your baby may not survive because the lungs are not fully developed. We've done almost everything we know to do so now we have to make a decision as to what to do next. We want to put you on some additional medication to develop the baby's lungs; this medication will require you to stay in the hospital until we are sure it's safe to send you home. We will have to give you shots in your hips every two days and strict bed rest is required for this medicine to work."

"How long is that", I asked. "Well, it's gonna take about six to eight weeks." Tears began to roll down my face. I didn't want to stay in the hospital that long. Smiley spoke up and said "Then that's just what we'll do." *We!*

Just then I looked at him like he was crazy and in addition, you know how people start to look to you when you're not in love with them anymore, every bump shows on their face, the nose is wide, the eyes are too far apart, the lips are big and the smile wasn't as cute anymore because some of the teeth look crooked now instead of straight; wavy hair looks knotty, so you know what I'm talking about.

Anyway, I think that I was somewhat a worrier. I was concerned that someone would find out about the abuse –more so than an actual care about what was happening to him, our marriage and our baby. I will attempt to explain here below:

Him, the spirit of abuse that had been transferred from his father to him (Smiley);

Our marriage – on the verge of Divorce – which is from my point of view;

Our baby?????

As I am lying there in my bed, I am thinking about

my life and how my decision would affect my unborn child. I thought about my past. *"Were the cigarettes I started smoking at age sixteen worth it? Were the abortions the reason why my uterus was so weak now? The alcohol – was my liver damaged? Smoking weed – how many brain cells had I really killed from my already educationally deprived brain?"*

I realize that I was deprived from the education I was offered; instead, like so many others, I took the other road; a road I was determined that my unborn child wouldn't go down when and if I ever got the opportunity to teach he or she about life.

From this moment on, I had decided and I was determined, in addition to promising God, that I will always praise my child; that I would constantly pray for my child; to give my child the things a child needs the most when growing up; the things I wanted and needed as a child. Don't get me wrong, I knew my parents loved me. I just can't recall hearing the phrase "I love you" much. I never lacked for anything materialistic, neither did my brother. See, it makes a difference in a child's life when they know *why* not to do it or something, instead of being **told *just don't do it.***

When your loved ones return home, that hug, that conversation of how their day was is not just for your husband or wife; it could literally make or break that child. Why not be the person who gives your child the right advice, instead of them getting the false information like I did. Why not talk to your child about other important things or something else other then get dressed – we have church tonight.

I called my mama to tell her what the doctor said and I began to cry even harder. I heard her say "Girl, get yourself together; you call me every day crying. I'm at work and I don't have time to deal with this. Whatever is gonna happen God has it under control. If it's meant for you to keep this baby, He'll bring it to pass." One thing I can say about my mama and my daddy --I never heard them doubt God. They believed God and stood strong on His promises. Nothing shook their faith. I believe, to this day, that's why they were so blessed.

Every night, while lying in bed, my hospital room door would open and there went my peace. Yep, it was him looking all dirty from his construction job and embarrassing me in front of the nurses. He would get dropped off at the hospital after work, take a shower, like he was a patient there (which was getting on my nerves), and then walk back home at about eleven o'clock every night. Yep, when it rains, it pours. Our Ltd (car) was broke down too.

So I prepared myself for the worse because I already knew he was already angry because of the car not working plus he had to walk home from the hospital, but guess what, I would be just fine if he didn't even come to the hospital, really, I would be just fine.

How has your day been? "What!" You care, I'm

thinking to myself. His reply would be "Ok" or "Good", which he would say very short and blunt. I'm gonna take a shower. I say "ok" and I am somewhat smiling because while you are in there showering, that gives me more time away from you. He's done within twenty minutes later. The water is turned off (Aww man, here we go.). He comes out, gets in bed as usual and takes up my space. He falls asleep, snores, drooling – which is everything that annoys me. Eventually, I lie down to get some sleep and then I'm awakened to him saying "I'm leaving now", with my eyes barely open. I said okay with a nod of my head. Thank you Lord was all I kept repeating when I finally knew he was really gone, no drama today. I would lie there watching TV and God begins to speak to me about my child that's growing inside of me. Speak to the baby and declare blessings not curses, life and not death. So I obeyed God so that I would not birth another me; the following list highlights the specifics I prayed:

-- This child will know God for him/herself.
-- This child will fear and reverence God.

-- This child will finish school.

-- This child will not get pregnant like I did if she's a girl.

-- This child will not get anyone pregnant before he is married, if a boy.

-- This child will be smart.

-- This child will not be addicted to any drugs or alcohol like the parents and their grandparents were.

-- This child will not be an abuser or get abused.

-- This child will live and not die, In Jesus' Name.

Just then I felt the strongest kick I had ever felt which scared me but at that scared but sacred moment, God says to me "well, did she receive that or what"? She? Yes, she. God said so clear. In the back of my mind I am still not focusing on what God can and will do. I started back watching TV again and in comes the nurse with the hip shot (Aww man, I hate this shot; it burns so bad) but I turned on over and took it in the hip which was the least sore area and dozed off to sleep shortly after that. That night I had the most beautiful dream. We were at a long table (we meaning the people who looked like Egyptians from the biblical days.) Here we are sitting, enjoying our feast with me pregnant and pretty too and with no one sitting beside me to make me hot and along comes this beautiful young girl with a special presence that you could feel just being around her. She comes and takes the empty seat next to me. I was mad at first, but only for a minute; this wasn't the only empty seat here but she took the one beside me (why, why, why). Now it's gonna get hotter than it already is but at least I had a little breeze. No, here you come; my mind was going on and on until she said "Hi, I'm Monchel; what's your name?" Just before I told her my name, I woke up. That was a weird dream I thought to myself. I then went to the bathroom and went back to sleep hoping it would come back. It didn't.

Lying there in bed with my hospital bedroom door open, I see a girl I went to college with walk by. "Jackie" I called out; she peeped her head in and said "girl, what are you doing here"? I turned right around and asked her the same question without answering her question to me. She said "I just had my baby; what did you have?" I got teary eyed and said "I'm here on bed rest; I haven't had my baby girl yet". "Oh, they told you what you were having already?" I said "No, God told me in a dream." "Really" she said, not really believing me. "Yes", I said with authority, believing what I said. "How's your son?" She looked at me crazy. "Did I tell you what I had?" I said "No, God told me while you were standing here; I heard him say boy (she had a boy)" now she believed. See, you don't have to argue your religion; just let God be God and the rest will take care of itself. He's fine, she said. We're going home in two days, she said and then asked how long do I have to be in here?" "Don't know" I said. "Can't go by what they say anymore; they told me six to eight weeks I've been here about three and a half weeks now, so I've placed everything in God's hands now. When it's time, I'll know it." Just then the nurse came in and that was just about time for Jackie's exit call, however, before she left, she asked me if I had a cigarette. I said "No, I quit when I found out that I was pregnant." "What! Girl, I don't know how you did it. I remember how much we used to smoke together." "I know" I said, "but I had to; didn't want the smoke in my baby's lungs. You kept on smoking while you were pregnant?" She replied "Yes". I thought to myself *"how selfish that was, but it didn't seem to matter to her what she had done to her baby. I promised I would always take care of mine."* My next two weeks went by fast and before I knew it, I was being discharged and on my way home.

Resting quietly on the couch later in the evening, in comes Mr. Frown. By now I had changed his name. In he comes, arriving home at 7:45pm but he gets off of work at 5:00pm and his job is only fifteen minutes away from the house; give or take a few minutes, dependent upon traffic he should have been home by 5:45pm at the very latest. But, anyway, he's here so what's to expect for this evening 'cause the last month was okay; no fighting, no fussing – just the lateness.

It had been almost two weeks of lateness but no fighting. Yeah, I was thinking (the same as you); well, it was a good sign huh, but not so fast. Bedtime came and so did the questions. So, can we have sex now or what? Rather than fight, I just said "come on man". So we could hurry up and get it over with. It didn't take long anyway, so what could it hurt, plus, I didn't want a head bunt or choke to come in on the scene. Afterwards, I take a shower and I noticed a warm flow that wouldn't stop, so I said to him, "wow that was a lot huh"; he says "No, it wasn't that much that came out." I said, well it's still running out" but then I dismissed it. We went to bed shortly thereafter. Couple of minutes later I felt this big gush and went to the bathroom. There was a clot in the commode so of course, I panicked and called my mama. I told her what I saw and she asked me what I had done (i.e., cleaning, bending, lifting something heavy, etc.). I told her I had done none of this, but we had just had sex. She said "What color is it girl?" I told her then she says "Sounds like your water broke. Go to the hospital now." It was about 10pm or so at night and I knew my husband had an early morning so I was scared to ask him to take me to the hospital (crazy huh?). Here I am, possibly in labor and scared to ask my husband to take me to the hospital. I told him what mama said and he said "Come on, let's go." I'm thinking to myself what's going on with this man; he's too nice, for a minute now, anyway. So, we arrive at the hospital and sure enough, that's what was going on – I'm in labor.

So, here I am now at the hospital and 4 cm dilated and moving fast so they were saying. They got me settled in and the nurse came in with a small bottle. She said we have to give all patients an enema (ha, ha; had heard my grandmother talk about them) but I had no idea what they felt like. The nurse begins to explain that I would have the urge to go to the bathroom shortly. How shortly – she didn't say, but seemed like as soon as she left I had to go. Now, here I am in the bathroom crying. My husband heard me so he opened the door and asked what was wrong. I told him I was scared to use the bathroom because she might fall in the commode so he went to get the nurse. She returned and came in to speak with me and to reassure me that it was normal to feel this pressure in that area so I did what I had to do and went back to my bed. At about three or 4 o'clock in the morning, WOW! Toothache pain is no way near the pain you experience when you're near delivery, but I was determined not to do the pain medication. I wanted this to be over with ASAP. Mr. Frowny was actually a big help so far. The nurse came in again to check on me --seemed like every thirty minutes or so. I was progressing well and so was the pain. About 6am or so, the doctor comes in to check on me; I was about to scream (but remained un-ghetto like). They took my husband out to prep him for the Delivery Room and I heard the doctor say let's get her in; she's about ready. The minute her head crowned I lost it. This was the worse I could ever imagine it would be. About 7:27am we welcomed her into the world, weighing in at 4 ½ pounds and 16 ½ inches long. Four pounds – are you kidding me. As much pain as I was in I thought she would be at least 8 to 9 pounds. Anyway, it was all over. I just wanted to rest a bit but then, here in comes the nurse with this baby so that she could be breast fed. I began to cry but I didn't know or understand why. My little girl finally latched on and I still had tears flowing down my face. Mr. Frowny had gone home to shower and change. As usual, he was a little late coming back to the hospital. Anyway, he came in and amazingly, he asked how I was doing and if there was anything that I needed or wanted. How many of you know that familiar spirits are sometimes not that far away, especially if they know you have an area of weakness. So I said to him "Yes I need something; I want a cigarette." "What! Are you serious?" "Yes I am serious; I am as serious as the pain that I just went through giving birth to your daughter, now give me one." He never stopped smoking, but he would go outside to take a smoke so as not to smoke around our baby. Anyway, I passed him the baby and went downstairs to smoke one from his pack of Newport. Well, I got downstairs but could not get back up. I was so dizzy and high from not smoking for nine months. I had to stay down there until this feeling leveled off. It finally did so I went back upstairs to find him, still holding the baby and looking down at her as if he still couldn't believe it. I thought to myself yeah, I can't believe she's here either; all of the abuse and torment you put me through. Then I got mad and walked over and took her from him while getting back in the bed to lay her on my chest and began to ponder how we were gonna leave him. About five hours later, my mom and dad walked in and that was the last time I held her that evening until visiting hours were over. Well now, after the delivery, you are generally in the hospital for not more than three days, if all is going well with both you and the baby, so I had two more days to go in this hospital.

The next day was the same old thing, tears and more tears, only I didn't want to feed her today. I was very sore and for her to latch on really hurt, but I pushed on; I figured if I could go through the labor pains I could go through this, so I pushed pass the tears and fed my baby girl. I couldn't understand how such a little thing ate so much. I didn't know if she was getting the pre-milk or if my milk had come in yet. We went on to sleep and woke up to the phone ringing which seemed like every hour, people were calling to say congratulations and ask the usual questions. Gee, my mama and his mama must have called everybody they knew to announce that Monchel was here. Later that evening, Mr. Frowny came in -- dirty as usual. I asked him,

"Did you wash your hands first before you pick up my baby." "Shut up, he said; she'll be alright. It's just a little dirt and dirt won't hurt or harm her. I used to eat dirt and so did you." I just stared him down and he finally went in the bathroom to take his shower.

The next day was terrible and for those of you who have breastfed – most of you know exactly what I mean. When she would latch on I thought I would scream but instead I just teared up. After I would nurse her both she and I would immediately fall off to sleep. When I woke up there she was, already wide awake, but she didn't make a sound. I'm thinking, this can't be so bad, but little did I know what was ahead of me. Now, here is the third day, and boy, am I ready to go home. Mama and Ms. Ella came and picked me up because of course Mr. Frowny had to work. When we arrived home, my little lady (Tootie) started up crying again so of course my mama became *mama* –and not grandmama. "Give her to me; she just wants to be held." I had already decided that I wouldn't spoil my baby by sitting around holding her all day because

I needed for someone to keep her while I was at work so I could make some money and get out of this life with Mr. Frowny. Tootie finally went to sleep and after hearing all the "what to do's" and "what not to do's", mama left and I laid down to take a nap. No sooner than I got to sleep well, there was a knock on the door. I go to the door and look out the peep hole and it was Ms. Fletcher, the older lady from upstairs. "I saw you come in and I just wanted to see the baby if it's okay?" "Of course", I said. See, Ms. Fletcher was more than good to me; she came down those stairs everyday just to see if I needed anything like food, something from the store, or just to give me a hug. She was Caucasian but one who didn't treat you like you were African American. At the same time she was there, my other neighbor (Beth) behind us who owned their own house and who the doctor told she would never have children, knocked on my back door (she and her husband had seen us getting out of the car too, evidently). They came bearing gifts -- a stroller and walker' I didn't know what to say or do. I had never seen this kind of generosity before from people who were not my own kind. Everybody volunteered to keep the baby if I had to go out, or cook dinner, or clean up. They were there for me to help with anything I needed because I was still recovering and I had to get quite a few stitches. I let each of them hold her but Beth held her the longest, just looking down at her in disbelief. My little one was a tiny thing. I let her hold her as long as she wanted to; I felt sorry for her that she couldn't conceive because of Multiple Sclerosis (MS).

Little Monchel was lying so comfortably in Beth's arms and I couldn't bear to tear her away, but I needed some rest while she was asleep. I gently took her from Beth and sent everybody home in a very warm and graceful manner. I went into the bedroom for both of us to lie down and get some rest. Finally, having closed my eyes, within 10-15 minutes later (wha, wha, wha – she started crying) was all I heard. *Oh no*, I thought; not already. I was getting depressed by the minute, so I tried feeding her –that didn't help; I tried rocking her –that didn't help; I tried talking and singing –that didn't help. I could not find the right solution so I just let her cry; after all, as the saying goes – the crying will help to strengthen her lungs.

Then, a few minutes later, I heard the key in the door and in walks Mr. Smiley. First thing he asks was "What's for dinner." Second thing he asks was "Why are you sitting there crying and what's wrong with her; shut her up, I'm tired. Look, I've had a long day at work and I gotta come home to no food and a crying baby. Give her to me!" So, he took her and put her in the car and took her for a ride, so he said. Anyway, she came back with him a couple of hours later and was sound asleep, and I still hadn't cooked. I had fallen asleep. He was definitely ticked off this time so I waited to see what would happen next. To my surprise, he rolled his eyes at me and said I'll be back and slammed the door. Guess what, yep! You guessed it! He woke her up before he left but at least she had stopped crying. So I made sure she was settled fine and I started to cook me something because I knew that by the time he came back home he would have already fed himself. Anyway, she was lying there for a while without crying and I was finally feeling this "Mommy" thing. It was about 8pm or so, then she started to cry again and I was like *Aww man; let's see if you can eat little girl.* She did and I just held her for about an hour and began to notice that every time she ate she would spit-up and quite a bit too. Then, she would squirm around like something was wrong or that she was not feeling well so the next day I called the doctor to let him know what was happening with her and he said to bring her in the very next day so that they could see what I was talking about. She was always fine during the morning hours; it was just in the evenings when she was at her worse, so the next day I called Smiley so he could get off work and of course he was angry but I didn't care; something was wrong with my baby and I needed to know what it was. Nevertheless, he came and we proceeded to go to the doctor. When we got there, the usual tests were done. Pricking her little finger for blood, weighing her, she was now 4lbs, 12 oz; not that much weight gain, which I knew she couldn't have gained any weight because she was spitting up everything she drank. The doctor came in and asked the usual questions. "How often are you feeding her?" I said "She's being fed every 4-6 hours." His response was "Well, that's normal.

All of her blood work is normal too, so let's try this. Feed her now and let's see if she keeps it down." *Okay it's a waiting game now*, I think to myself. Right on cue with her burp it all comes back up. So then he says "Mom, what are you eating and drinking?" I said "Meat, vegetables and juice and some soda, but not that much." "Are you drinking any alcohol?" "No, no" I responded. What about tobacco?" "Yes", I replied. "I started back smoking." "That's one of the problems" he said, condescendingly. "Babies don't like to smoke cigarettes. When you smoke, so does she; it comes through your milk." "Wow! I didn't even think about that, so that's why she's not keeping the milk down." "Well, now that's one of the reasons probably", he said. "The other reason I think is because she is lactose intolerant, so we're gonna put her on a soy based milk, called Enfamil ProSobee Formula and see how that goes. That doesn't mean that you should keep smoking though. The second hand smoke still affects her lungs and you don't want to give her Asthma, do you? And, I'm also gonna treat her for colic; I think she is very gassy. Let's see you back for your six week checkup and we'll for from there." I was so relieved that it wasn't anything serious and also relieved that I could still smoke (outside of the house, of course). Now, when I think back on it, how stupid was my thought – relieved that I could still have a cigarette. Wow!

Anyway we went to the grocery store with a WIC voucher to get her milk and other things and then we drove on home.

As usual, when we arrive home, he went on in and showered, dressed to go out and left. This bothered me but didn't bother me at the same time, if that makes sense. This would give me some peace, at least until she started up crying again, which was happening quite a bit. I allowed the crying to continue, but I turned her over on her side and propped her up on pillows. She still did a lot of squirming so I picked her up and laid her belly over my leg and patted her and bounced her a little, at the same time, which seemed to help her a little bit. That was the only way I knew to help my baby get rid of some of this gas on her belly. She fell asleep after all of her little pain was somewhat gone. I couldn't really tell if the colic drops were helping or not, but I just rolled with it. What to fix for dinner was the next concern. I pulled out the pots and pans to make a quick meal, which would be macaroni and cheese, baked chicken and canned string beans. It had been a while since he last put his hands on me so I thought I would be a good wife and take care of my domestic duties.

I had prepared our dinner for several hours now and, well, guess what? This man stayed out until about 9:15pm. I was trying hard to be the dutiful wife and have everything prepared by the time he came home. Well, dinner was cold and I put it in the refrigerator, picked her up from her crib and got in the bed. She seemed to sleep better in my bed (my parents bought it, so I figured it was mine). I laid her on her side along with me on mine, held her close to me and we fell asleep. Well, about two hours later I felt a hand rubbing on my thigh. I think to myself, *Oh no; are you serious?* So I said, "Man, you know I can't have sex until my six week checkup." I said "I am not trying to get pregnant by you again." I said "Already our little Tootie is a handful." Of course, all he heard was *"by you"*. The next thing I know I was being drugged out of bed by my hair and raped on the floor. He was so rough he ripped two of my stitches out, which burned me badly. I had to sit in a soothing bath of water. Once I was done with that I grabbed the phone and called his mama. Again, notice I said his mama (never mine). I couldn't call my parents and tell them none of this. I was determined to not hear the words "I told you so" from them. You might ask, but how could those words come from them? Well, when they insisted on us getting married, amazingly, they had forgotten about all and what was said when they first found out I was pregnant. Yeah, forgot all about it. We had decided to get married is what they were telling the church folk. Anyway, I could hear his mama on the other end, talking to him, after I told her what he had done. She was yelling and cursing him out "Boy, I done told you not to put your hands on that girl no more. Let her alone while she just had a baby and still bleeding and all; you can kill her by doing that. Her body has had a baby for you and you want to have sex with her before she can have it; she'll probably get pregnant again. She can get pregnant now real easy. You better hope she is okay!" I can hear him saying "I'm sorry mama." But now I am thinking, *"But mama, what about apologizing to me?"* I never did get one; he just left me alone (conversation and all) for what seemed like forever. Six weeks came and the doctor came in with results of my urine and the baby's blood work. The baby was fine but she was still very gassy. His mama had told us we needed to move there so she could take care of Tootie (which was now her nickname, given to her by my father). I really wanted to move there, but not for that reason but for safety reasons. The doctor said "Well, there's good news and better news. You've healed very well and, you're pregnant also. I could hear the pen drop; that's how silent it was in the room. Smiley was looking like he had just been slapped real hard which is what I saw in my head happening. So, I guess we're in this for another nine months. The doctor proceeded to tell us that the nurse will schedule my appointments and they will watch this pregnancy very close too. *I don't think so*, I said to myself. *I am not having this baby.*

We returned home and immediately called his mama and told her she was right; I'm pregnant. She was happy and said "Now you guys have to move on down here so I can help you." I still can't believe it. I was so depressed that when the baby cried I did too; again and again.

Well sometime between now and before I started working again, yes, I did abort the second baby by Smiley. He was in agreement, eventually, not to have the pregnancy continued.

We told everybody we were moving and Ms. Beth just cried, cried and cried. "Oh my, what will I do with you guys no longer living here!" We had somewhat become best friends since Tootie had been born. I saw her every day; I do mean every day.

She had to hold Tootie every single day. She never knew about what was happening behind closed doors and she also did not know that I was expecting another baby. We had a going away dinner for us, which was very hard for me. Ms. Fletcher had gotten sick and admitted to the hospital so I didn't see her before we left. Ms. Beth and Alan acted like we were their kids leaving home for the first time and like they would never see their kids again. We pulled up to Tidewater Drive in the yellow Ltd and with suitcases in hand, moved in. So we have his mother, him, me, his baby sister, two brothers, Baby Tootie and our new baby on the way. His mama lived in a three bedroom apartment, plus there was another sister who didn't live there but was there all the time with all her kids. His mama kept them during the day. The apartment was always crowded.

I started applying for jobs immediately and finally got one working at the mall in a men's store selling suits. I was quite good at it; I always had good fashion sense so my check was okay. Smiley went to work with his father who owned his own business and he, Smiley's father, would occasionally stop by with fruits and vegetables (as if that would make up for him leaving my mother in law for another woman) maybe twice a month. You could clearly see that his mama still cared for him and hated him all at the same time.

So now, today is my day to work again. I am actually beginning to love this job; the only thing I hated was this bus ride to and from work, however *I did pretty good tonight*, I thought to myself, as I was walking out of the door, heading to the Bus Stop, but I didn't even realize that the bus I saw pulling away was mine until I reached the bench. I'm thinking, *I have no phone to call him to come pick me up and the next bus wasn't due to come for another 45 minutes.* Sitting there watching the cars go by and thinking about my day when a car pulls up and asks do I need a ride. "Nope", I said "but thanks anyway though". I didn't even give him a second thought until I felt someone's hands around my neck from behind, pulling me away from the Bus Stop and into a car. I was screaming for help with all my might until he burst me upside my head so hard I had to shut up. He then threw me inside his car and sped off. In my mind I knew what was going to happen so I just began to pray that he wouldn't kill me. We ended up at this construction site beside a hospital (yep, a hospital). I just sat there and waited for him to get out on his side. While he was telling me "I'm not gonna hurt you, just do what I say and you'll be okay." As soon as he opened his door, I opened mine and ran; didn't get very far though before he tackled me and then ripped off my stockings. My hands were tied together and he began to pull my panties down. I really freaked out then and screamed as loud as I could. This time he hit me so hard my head felt like it was embedded in the dirt. He did what he had intended to do; got up and walked away as if we knew each other and said "See you later lil lady." As soon as he got to his car he turned and looked at me again and said "I can't leave you like that can I?" He came back over, wiped the dirt off my face and picked me up and threw me in this hole at the site. I heard the car pull away and I began to crawl and scream my way out of this hole. Two angels walked by and heard me, pulled me out, took me to the hospital and stayed with me until the police and my husband arrived. Of course questions were asked and tests were done. My husband finally arrived and instead of holding me and saying it's going to be alright, the question he asked instead was "Do you know this guy? Have you been helping him in the store? Was there a chance that he thought maybe there was more to you and him?" "What! No, I've never seen this guy before, but I tell you this; I will never ever forget his face." After all of the tests and questions were complete I was finally able to leave. We get in the car and Then, I'm asked "How could you be so stupid not to pay attention to your surroundings and not see that someone was near you to grab you like that?" There was absolutely no consoling; none whatsoever, just criticizing; and the criticism continued once we were in the house. So much so to the point that his mama said "Shut up boy; you don't know what this girl has been through. Go upstairs baby; your bath water is waiting for you." My mother in law helped me get undressed, put me in the tub, washed me and combed the dirt out of my hair, with me crying at the same time. She then began to explain how she knew what I was feeling. The same thing had happened to her at a much younger age, so she somewhat knew what I was feeling. I sat in the tub for what seemed like an eternity, and then I slowly got out of the tub and prepared myself for bed.

Later, in the wee hours of the morning, I woke up to Smiley's hands feeling on me. I said "Have you lost your mind? You can't be serious, or are you crazy?" "Yes I am serious" was his reply. "I'm horny." "Well", I said "I'm emotionally distraught right now; can't you see that?" "Yeah, I see it and the only way you're gonna get over this is to make love to your husband." Yeah, I went along and did the normal thing and laid there, thinking to myself *"what kind of man is this who cares nothing about his wife being raped and beaten, and on the same night this happens to her he then asks her to have sex; this sure was not making love. It's like this was a turn-on for him or something; like it was a movie for him or something. Sick is what this is; I hated him even more now than I ever did before."* But, nonetheless, I stayed. I was still determined that I wasn't going back home to mom and pop.

My attacker was eventually caught and the trial begins and ends, quickly. I was his fifth victim; he is now behind bars where he should be. Oh, did I mention he had a girlfriend and he was also impotent. According to his attorney, this is what made him do these rapes – his impotency. Yeah, right!

Now, with this behind me I was focused on raising my baby and still saving up enough money to get away from this man. A beautiful spring day brought out people, kids, insects and everything you could imagine; even ex-girlfriends. HA! I am now noticing Smiley walking a little more than usual; supposedly his ex is waiting on his sister to get off. They are supposed to be going somewhere, but let's get back to this walking he's doing. I'm in the bedroom with baby Tootie when something says to me go into the kitchen. So, I do. As I am coming around the corner he grabs this piece of paper from his sister's girlfriend and throws it in the trash. I'm a good pretender so of course I didn't see it. Smart enough to wait until everyone leaves the kitchen. Then I go back through the trash. Yes, the trash can. I find what I'm looking for. On a piece of paper towel, bald up, that says *I miss you; when can I come and see you again? Miss you too* -- was her response, but she never got to answer the rest. I interrupted. Oh yeah, I couldn't wait to burst his bubble. I intentionally waited until everybody got home and approached him with the piece of paper towel. I didn't have to say a word; I just threw it at him. If eyes could pop out of one's head and go back in, his would have done so right then and there. Of course, everyone else was wondering what it was and I felt empowered at that moment while also thinking about my repercussions for later when we were alone. "Yeah, yeah" his reply was, "This don't mean nothing; I was just joking." "Just joking" I said. "I didn't hear either one of you laughing about it." A smirk came on his face. "It was just a joke girl." Then he brushed it off, like it never happened. "I'm leaving you" was my reply. "Where are you going?" he asked. "Home, to my parents" I said. He then replied "I told you it was a joke." "Yeah" I said, a joke; I'm going to show you what's funny. Let's see who's laughing later. I went into our bedroom and closed the door. His mama came in, as usual and said "Baby, give him another chance. I just finished talking to him and he really regrets writing that note." I looked at her and said "Ma, the only thing he regrets is getting caught." She continues, saying "I know my son loves you baby; I've never seen him like this with anyone but you. He slipped a bit; just give him another chance." So I told her I would think about it. What I was really thinking about was what he was gonna do to me later when everyone had gone to bed. Finally, night rolls around and I had already prepared myself for the head bunt, choking or hair pulling. To my surprise, neither one happened. Just an apology and I love you and good night, which left me to ponder what I was really gonna do. Things were good for a month or so, then for some reason he just decided to go into the military. Back home we went, after 1 ½ years and moved into a trailer home. Basic training was over and we're getting into the groove of this military lifestyle; waiting for housing when the Somalia war came. After a long while, he came home and told me he would be gone for at least six months; he was commuting back and forth from where he was stationed every two days or so. We rarely saw each other, which was a good thing for our marriage, so it seemed. Two months into Somalia, I'm driving his car to church to meet my mama so that we can attend a musical church event, which was down the street from her house. Baby girl (Tootie) accidentally kicks the glove compartment of the car as we are pulling in to park and out falls pictures of some girl in a nigh tie and in a swim suit. This is totally inappropriate for him to have. I lost it right there in the parking lot and cursing on church ground. I picked them up and put them in my purse and proceeded to find my mama, who had saved us seats. I handed them to her and she asked "Who is this?" "I don't know, I said; I just found them in the glove compartment of his car." "Oh", she said and quickly dismissed them as probably being nothing. Smacking my lips I took them back from her and sat there thinking what I could do about them with him being so far away. Wait for the call and bust him I thought. When the call came I didn't say a word. See, I'm still planning my get away in my head.

"Military Boy Toy"

Now about this time, I am working as a secretary in a middle school; they say it pays to know somebody. My parents knew someone in every place seemed like. We always had good jobs. While mentoring a few girls, I became close with one who would cling to me every day after school. I would, from time to time drop her off at home since it was on my way. One day she asked me to come in to her home and meet her brother who was home on leave, so I did. Can you say instant attraction?

From that day on we were inseparable. He would spend all day and night with me. I even introduced his friend to my friend and they started to fool around. We fell in love quick; so quick I had introduced him to my mama very early on -- yes my mama. I told her I was leaving Smiley for him and we were gonna get married. Then she said "Girl, this boy is five years younger than you; what and how can y'all survive?" I brushed off her questions and told her that we will be okay. Before I knew it those six months came and went by real fast and hubby was due home. Not to mention the fact that my new lover --my boy toy had been AWOL for the last five months. Yeah, I put something on him; I had learned a little from being with different guys. Not enough to keep him from straying in the end though, and not before I found out that I was pregnant. OH MY GOSH! These three letters were not out back then so Oh My God were words I used and a few choice ones to go along with it. Now I *had* to leave Smiley; he would kill me if he knew I had gotten pregnant by another man. So now its two weeks until the time Smiley gets home and I'm in Winn-Dixie (I miss those stores) shopping and I fainted. They rushed me to the hospital where I found out they were gonna rush me into emergency surgery. One of my tubes had ruptured; the pregnancy was in my tube and poison was going into my blood stream.

After the surgery, a few days later, I woke up to find my friend, my cousin, my mama and my aunt looking kind of worried while waiting in my room. I had already told the doctor beforehand that nothing was to be discussed in front of anyone but me so they couldn't get any information. Of course I was sleeping a lot; I know there were some nosy bodies asking questions as to what happened.

I told them I had a cyst that had ruptured and we never spoke about it again. By then, my boyfriend had been found and was sent back to his unit and that was the end of us. Love ain't love when you're cheating; it just feels that way at the time.

1 Thess. 5:22 "Abstain from all appearance of evil." (KJV)

"Cracka Lackin"

I am now enjoying me. I am working at a school but then a reality check kicks in; it's not enough to sustain me. So my mama makes me go to cosmetology school. At first I hated it a lot, but then it starts to feel natural to me so I hang in there. Beginning my second week of school I'm on the floor because they found out who my mama was. My days consisted of the following: Work school day from 7a to 1p; shop was from 1:30p to 5:30p and school was from 6p to 9p. Yes, I was tired but I hung in there. I came to my mama's shop the next day. She always made me bring my mannequin to her shop. She was also an instructor so I had two teachers. Her question to me today was "How was school? My answer to her was "great"! "I'm on the floor now and I did a haircut and curl last night." "What! You're not supposed to be on the floor yet. You have to do 300 hours before you're on the floor. What kind of mess are they doing over at that school? Oh no, you are coming away from there. I will put you in Mitchell's." Sure enough, she withdrew me and asked for her money back. At first they tried to buck her but after she threatened to call State Board on them about me being on the floor too soon, they then had no problem with it, no problem whatsoever. She says "That's what I get for trying to support a black school." So, to Mitchell's we go.

Early on at Mitchell's I begin to hate going. I hated my teacher and I hated the atmosphere, but not until I met my God brother. We'll call him Tim. Tim and I became closer than close. (Hey, watch it! Not close like that.) See, he's gay. Although I did ask him if he had ever been with a woman because if not, I was gonna try to convert him, but he was a pretty man. Anyway, school was fun and interesting again.

Finger waves! I hate these things. Everything else came so easy to me. It was in my genes. The C shaping was getting on my nerves. Two weeks later my teacher was out for the day, so the substitute teacher told us to pull out our mannequins and work on finger waves. Yep; I cut up as usual; frustration had really set in that night. I didn't get any weed for us to smoke before class so I was ill. I pulled out my mani and started talking to myself. "No weed and she want me to do finger waves." A few extra choice words came out that I'd rather not say, but as I was combing my mani's hair, guess what? It began to take shape. Yep, those C's, row by row began to form and I was elated. This was the only style that had been a challenge for me, but finally, I conquered it.

My God brother and God sister hung in there, cutting, styling, coloring – no problem for them. Weave, wigs, no problem. Creating a piece of hair to look like a flower, ice, fountain – no problem. Fantasy hair was my forte. Hair show after hair show we won. Top salon in our city year after year, and I'm still not finished with school yet. I was good at this hair thing so I made good money. My God sister was my best model. She was also a shampoo-stylist at a shop, along with one of my girlfriends. They would always be the main feature of our hair shows. The show stoppers we called them. Ice Queens, Mermaids, Flower Pots, Wine Bottles -- my mind was endless when it came to fantasy hair. I would dream of different things to create. My sister Vicky would always be willing to let me do whatever I wanted. I loved it. So, we are now preparing for one of the biggest hair shows ever on a military base. Of course it is sold out and, after that, the club. It's what my God brother, my God sister Vicky and I did –we modeled. This was against my mama's wishes, of course. The "D" Club was the hottest spot, so we're driving to the spot; you know we have to get our weed first. We stop by the "man's" house; what, he's out! On to the next "man's" house (his wasn't as good so he was 2nd on the list). What, he's out too! Now, heading to the third man on the list who lived around the corner; he was out too. What's going on? City had a big bust on weed so it was "dry" as they called it. Aww man, I don't even wanna go to the Club now was my mental state. Okay, then we all figure out what we gonna do after this dry spell. Well, everyone went on home except me. A few minutes later, one of the lead models and one of my models who had become a good friend said she got one more spot she could try, so we did. She came out smiling so I knew she scored. What she had scored wasn't revealed until we had gone into her house. She had three empty soda & water bottles, a plate, some foil and the ash tray. We sat down at the table she fixed up for us; she put holes in the bottles and on each side she placed foil with holes on top and passed them out to us. Then she proceeded to tell us "Go ahead and light your cigarettes. We gonna need the ashes." I'm thinking to myself, *wow, this must be some good weed if we gonna smoke it like this; this is new for me.* I'm smoking my cigarette and she goes in her pocket, pulls out this plastic bag with what looked like a sugar cube in it, puts it on the plate and cuts it up. "Woe! What kind of weed is that girl", I asked. "Girl, this ain't no weed, this is the good stuff; its crack." I sat my bottle down and looked at her like she was crazy. "I don't do no crack girl; you seen them crack heads we just passed? I'm not doing that." She looked me dead in my eye and said "Do I look like them? I do it." I was in utter shock. When I say this was one of the prettiest females I had ever seen, I mean it. No, she didn't look like a crack head so I thought to myself, I'll try it; it can't hurt. The last thing she said to me before she showed me how to inhale this bottle was the key to this – you control you. Oh, ok. I'm good then. Took a toke and oh my gosh, it was the best feeling I had felt; it was better than sex and weed.

I think we spent about $300 bucks between us that night until daylight came in. So we made this a weekly event between us three and nobody knew; not even Vicky or Tim. Tim eventually found out because I got high with him one day, but then I eventually felt guilty for doing this. I could see it took an effect on him. He wasn't coming to school as much and he was cursing out our teacher at school more and more, until one day she sent him home and he never came back. The man can still do some hair though. Bootleg, that is; he has his own shop in his house. Vicky was never told. I knew she would be disappointed in me. She was like the sister to me my mama never birthed.

Smoking crack once a month became twice a month; twice a month became once a week and once a week became every day; then, every day became all day, when possible. My other two partners and I had fallen out by this time. I was getting tired of being the one to only put up the money we needed for our high so I left them alone and went on my own. I had to be sure the man had seen my car enough to sell to me by now. Yep, no problem, except for the night he was out and I had to cruise the "block" and found me this crack head named Ree Ree and asked her if she knew where I could score. Sure, she said, but we have to go to his house. I know your question is --a stranger? Yes, a stranger was in my car and a crack head at that. Wait, what am I saying? I'm a crack head now, but still not admitting it, even though I was losing weight and had the same ponytail in my head for about two months now; shampoo (no), but gel every day (yes). Nasty! That's what it was; face was still made up and I was still working and smoking all night when I could. Smoking so much at night I would get my baby up out of bed in the dead cold, throw her in the backseat of the car, speed down the road to get this thing that was driving me now. Some nights Smiley would be home so I didn't have to wake her up. I would sneak out and be back in before he knew it and I would smoke in the bathroom. Smiley slept so hard he wouldn't know if a gunshot went off in the house. You literally had to shake him and sometimes slap him to get him to wake up. I enjoyed the slapping times (Ha! Ha! Ha!). Still functioning, one morning I went to drop my baby off for kindergarten at school and as usual little Tootie was late again, but at least I brought her to school. Her teacher, Ms. Cee, asked me if she could speak to me. We stepped out in the hall and she began to tear up and say "I spoke with the principal yesterday. They wanted to keep your daughter back in kindergarten for another year because she's missed so many days, but I convinced her not to because it's not your baby's fault; it's yours. I asked her not to penalize the child; she's a good student and smart, but that you were on drugs (crack) and you need help and that I was going to try my best to help you." "What!" I looked at her and said, "I'm not on no drugs." "Oh yes you are" she said; "you look just like my husband". "I've been through this before. I know what it looks like and you need help." I stood there and cried like a baby and promised her I would get help, and in exchange, she wouldn't tell my mama (who did her hair).

<u>James 1:17</u> "Every good and perfect gift is from above, coming down from the Father of the heavenly lights, who does not change like shifting shadows."

As soon as I left her I went to Ree Ree's house with my bottle in my hand and we laughed about it and got high, as usual. By this time I knew all the drug dealers who sold that, but I wasn't functioning at work or school. So, I lost my job at the junior high school for calling out all the time. They knew something was up but didn't know what I was on. I had to get some money from somewhere other than the shop. Oh yeah, cosmetology school was done too but my mother didn't know. I still pretended like that's where I was going every evening I left home. So, one day a sheriff comes to my house looking for me because my husband called the shop and told me. That was on a Saturday. I paid him no attention. Monday they came and got my behind from the house and locked me up on a warrant for a stolen vehicle (SUV) that I had rented from my drug dealer and his buddies for my drugs. Yeah, they totaled it, wrapped it around a telephone pole after a police chase in another town next to ours. So I am now in jail; Aww man! How am I gonna explain this. I called my mama and father to bail me out and lied and told them it was one of my client's brothers who I rented the SUV from and he got scared and ran after the police chase. I thought the vehicle had been turned in with no problems. They didn't know that I had rented the vehicle in exchange for the drugs. I was bailed out and fussed out. This still didn't stop me. I had begun writing checks now at the grocery stores. $51.49 was the total. Fifty dollars it cost for my crack and $1.49 for my cigarettes. Three and four grocery stores per day I would hit, knowing I didn't have the money to cover this check. Now Walmart had just opened and they didn't have me in their NSF system yet so I hit them a couple of times until one night, I noticed they were taking a long time. This was probably my third trip to them for the day. $51.49! A police car pulled up and out gets this officer who I knew and he knew my parents and the situation with the SUV. He comes in, looks at me, he takes the check I gave them and takes me outside and says "Look at you. Get some help girl. Do I need to call your mama and daddy so we can get you the help you need. I do this every day; you're on that stuff. Do not write another check at any grocery store or I will lock you up myself. Go home, now!" He took the check and tore it up. I watched him as he went back in the grocery store and talked with the manager. I could see her shaking her head, almost as if she felt sorry for my situation. The next day pawn shops became my friend. I pawned all of my jewelry. That money lasted three days. The fourth day came and I needed another plan. Saturday rolls around and I thought, *Hmm, I have the joint bank card, but I knew better than to touch our bills, food, rent money.* So I thought he (hubby) was never home anymore anyway so he wouldn't know. Yeah, the signs of cheating were there again. I didn't care. I had me a new boyfriend and crack was his name. I figured out what I needed to do. I would go to the teller window, withdraw money, go to another teller, get a deposit slip/envelope and act like I'm depositing money in the account. That way he wouldn't see a change in the account if he was monitoring it. Wow! I was good, so I thought to myself.

Then, one day, my cousin came home on a surprise visit. She took one look at me and said, "Oh my goodness! You're on that stuff. Oh no! We are gonna get you some help TODAY!" Mind you, I still had the same ponytail in my head for three months after I started using cocaine. I would take a rag, wipe the old gel out and put new gel on the curl; on the top I would tie it up while I'm riding around or working. Huh! It still looked good to me, but not to my cousin though. She looked at my head and said "Look at your hair; look at your bones. You mean to tell me nobody can see what's going on here with this girl. Come on, we are gonna talk to Smiley together. I told her she would have to wait until the evening, so she left and came back way before it was time for me to get off. By that time my mama wasn't working as much so she had me to run the shop and she had started working for the State Board as an examiner, so I basically ran her shop now. I remember thinking out loud one day and I said to mama, as we were walking to our cars so she could follow me to my house. "Mama, he probably will really beat me now" I said to her. "Oh no, we won't be having none of that." She opened her purse and revealed her little pistol she carried and said "You will be okay."

We got to the house and walked in. I sat down and she began to ask him. "Have you looked at your wife lately?" His response is "We don't ever really see each other that much. You know I'm still commuting and she's never really here so to answer your question, no, I haven't." "Look at her man; can't you see she's on that stuff and bad." My mama began to cry. She said, "It only took one look for me and I knew. How could you not know? Look at her hair; she would always keep her hair fly. You can see her ribs -- the bones in her cheeks. She needs help." He looked over at me and stood up. She looked up at him and patted her purse and said "You know I got my help with me. You won't be doing that this evening. We need to get her some help and right now." Again, he looked at me and asked me did I want help. I shook my head yes and he said okay. He hugged me, she hugged us and then she left, but not without reminding him about her purse. I think she was the only one I had ever seen who could scare him off. She called me the next few days and said she was flying back to Georgia and that she knew I could do this and that she truly loved me.

I chilled for about a week and went right back to the rugged course I was now on. Not quite as bad, but I was smoking all day.

Matthew 12:45 "Then it goes and takes with it seven other spirits more wicked than itself, and they go in and live there. And the final condition of that person is worse than the first. That is how it will be with this wicked generation."

I did one whole week of nothing but smoking. No sleep; no sleep whatsoever. No food, no water. Yes, I stayed up seven days, seven nights and on the eighth day my body finally gave way to the drug and I fell asleep. I woke up to a knock on my crack girlfriend's door. She was never a girlfriend, just a house to smoke at when my husband was home. Answering the door still high, I looked and saw who it was and opened it. Now here he (Smiley) sees a plate of crack crumbs on the table along with her pipes and my bottle. He was so mad he overlooked everything. He had come to tell me that the Sheriff had been to our house again and that he had a warrant for my arrest again; this time for worthless checks. I looked at him and said okay, I'll go turn myself in again. As soon as he left I started smoking what I had left on the plate. I knew I would probably not be bailed out this time by my parents, so I needed the rest of this high. To my surprise, my parents were already at the Sheriff's office when I got there. Straight to the holding cell I went and waited for them to bail me out. I waited, and waited and waited. The sun went down and I was still waiting. "Okay, what's going on" I asked the guard standing by my cell. "What do you mean?" she asked. I asked her "What was taking so long for the bail out to take place" (listen at me sounding like a criminal). She went to check and came back and told me there was no bail. "Your parents are gone." She then walked away. I know she didn't just say they were gone and that I was still here. What! She has got to be telling me a lie. I know my parents didn't leave me here, and if they did, that means I'm gonna be in here overnight. Wow! I'm seriously locked up now. I began to realize the seriousness of my situation now and the tears began to flow and my high was gone and I do mean GONE. Jail, I have never been in jail. Yeah, a holding cell, but never a jail. I was raised better; to know better than to get myself in trouble enough to be in this situation. Overnight, on a steel mattress or what felt like one, I woke up to the clanking of keys and doors. They were coming to get us to take us to court. I would finally find out everything that was going on. When they first brought me in they just said worthless checks and fraud. I get to court in this ugly green jumpsuit, no makeup and this same ponytail with no gel in it today. My mama took one look at me and just begins to weep; my father just looked at me and hung his head. They called my case.

Charges are as follows:
1 count vehicular destruction
56 counts of worthless checks
56 counts of fraudulent checks
30 counts of fraudulent deposits

Total Cost:

$5,500 SUV

$6,000 worthless checks

$6,000 fraudulent checks

$2,000 fraudulent deposits

Can you say almost $20,000 worth of craziness; *girl, I have no words to describe this craziness you have done* was the look my daddy gave me. The judge looked at me and asked "How do you plead to these charges, Mrs. Smiley?" "Guilty" I said. "Sir, I'm guilty." "Mrs. Smiley, your parents don't look like the type of people that would teach you to do something like this; what happened to you?" "Your Honor, Sir, I just fell on hard times and I had to have this money to take care of me and my child." "Mrs. Smiley, this type of activity is not just for you and your child needing things. I've been doing this a long time; this looks like drug use activity charges. Am I right, Mrs. Smiley?" "Yes, your Honor; I have a real bad weed problem and I would lace it sometimes with cocaine." "Oh, ok Mrs. Smiley". He looked down at his paperwork and said

"Wow!" I'm not gonna make you pay all these worthless check fees. The grocery stores kept letting you write the checks and knew you were a bad customer. Now, as for the bank fees of $2,000, $9,500 restitution is to be paid and you receive 2 years of supervised probation, along with 200 community service hours and mandatory narcotics anonymous classes. Gavel hits the table/pulpit where he's sitting.

Yeah, I told the judge a lie. I couldn't let my parents know what I was really doing. Notice I still haven't mentioned my husband, Mr. Smiley. He was not there during either jail incident (only there to say Sheriff is looking for you and then he was gone.) Gone back to his girlfriend or whatever he was doing when he wasn't home.

So I am clean now, right? (Yeah, it's a month), all the while thinking every single day about getting high but I just needed to play this role again. I did my community service in the public library which was filing all these books, answering the telephone and other tasks as assigned. Then, reporting to my probation officer for the supervisory probation hours, as the judge ordered, but I still spoke to my get-high partner every other day, taking her advice. "Girl, do your court ordered months of probation because they are gonna drug test you; you have to get through that then you will be good." So the next six months were good for me. I was back in school, community service was done, probation almost over, marriage was okay, bills were paid and money was back in accounts at the bank. Things were looking up. Probation period was up and I was actually clean. So, I went out to the club to celebrate and guess who I run into? Yep, Ms. Pretty and of course, she asked how I was and what were my plans for later because she was gonna hook up with *the man* and he had some good stuff too. "Girl nah, I'm done with that. I went to hell and back with that stuff." "I'm so sorry that happened to you girl, but I told you from the beginning that you have to control it and not let it control you." We then hugged each other and got on the dance floor. Later that evening, the last call for alcohol came and I walked around looking for her. Yeah, I thought about what she said the whole time while we were in the club. I walked up to her and said "You still gonna see *the man?*" Yeah, people I know - I know. I was convinced that I could control it and not let it control me. After the club, I stopped by the store to get me a soda – specifically for the bottle and I met her at her house. We smoked all night until the morning. Once again, I was in this drug whirlwind just like that.

It had been a month and I had left her alone and had gone back to the old crack friend's house to smoke. By this time her cousin (who was a fine young thang) had started selling so he would come by the house quite often. We began making eye contact with each other and sometimes he would throw an extra rock in my bag. One day we were sitting at her house just chilling and in walks Mr. Tim. "What's up ladies" and his eyes go directly to me. He knew I was different than the other crack heads he dealt with (so I thought to myself). He had come to drop us off some smoke. He was just about to leave, but before he left he called me into the kitchen and said, "Say girlie, I been checking you out and I like what I'm seeing. "What's up wit ya"? "What you mean" I asked. "You know what I'm saying girlie; you ain't gotta buy this stuff. Let's hook up and I'll give you what you need when you need it." This crossed my mind for a minute (a minute) then I said "No thanks". "That would mean I'm just like the other ones you deal with, just not on a bad looking level." "Okay, I get it and I respect you for that. So, since you won't let me get wit ya, I need to borrow your car and I give you $100 worth of my stuff." "Sure", I said. That was $100 worth of free crack; I would be crazy not to take that deal. I gave him the key and waited for him to get back from his pickup to re-up on his dope.

I waited, and waited and waited. Finally, the phone rang and they asked for me so my girlfriend (real friend) hands me the phone and it's the police asking me did I loan Mr. Tim my car? "Yes", I said. "It's okay that he is driving it." "Oh, okay" the police is saying to someone else in the room. She gave him permission to drive the car. The other voice comes through the phone and it's my daddy's voice. I lost my breath. "Tell her I said she better be here at this house in five minutes or I'll be there where she is in two minutes. "Oh, no, what just happened? I made it to Mr. Tim's house in three minutes, tops. Now, here is my aunt, my brother and the police, looking at me like I was crazy. I could hear my daddy saying "Girl, you had better get in the car and get over here now." My brother drove behind us and my aunt behind him. We pulled into my dad's driveway and it looked like the family reunion was at his house -- not early but very late at night.

We walk into the house and both grandmas, all aunts that lived there were there and my husband (What!) and my mama who wouldn't even look at me, along with my God sister Vicky whose tears wouldn't stop flowing from her eyes.

My dad looked at me and said "Go take a bath and let me know when you're done." I looked at him and said "Take a bath, for what? I already did that today." "No, he said very sternly. "Go take a bath in my holy tub back there girl." I went and did what he said and came back to the conference room (living room). He told me to go back into the bedroom. "For what" I asked, smugly. What you gonna do, spank me?" "Girl, don't play with me; get to the bedroom." We went into the bedroom, him, my mama and me. "Take those clothes off. I'm gonna check you." "Check me, for what", I asked. "Needle marks girl." "Daddy, I don't shoot drugs, I smoke them." "Don't care girl, take them off. I'm gonna check you and check me he did. He checked every crevice and crack. Here I am 27 years old and my father is looking at my naked body; 27 years old. I'm actually fully unclothed --naked in front of my daddy and my mama. After he was done I was made to sit in front of everyone and explain myself, but not before Mr. Smiley got up and said "I'm gonna let you all deal with this. I'm done with your daughter. We just received an eviction notice. We have lost our house; she's run through our bank account again in a matter of two months; they have been calling for her car but they just couldn't find it. I'm done with her" and he walked out.

Why and how could I do this to the family were the two main questions from my daddy. My mama still had not said a word; just shedding tears all evening. "How could you embarrass the family like this? You do know what these church folks are gonna say, right?"

That's the problem with this family, I thought to myself. *Always worried and concerned about what the church folks are gonna say. Church folk act like drugs and alcohol don't have a name on them just because you're a preacher's kid. The enemy, Satan, don't care who he destroys, Christian and non-Christian alike.*

I just replied to them that "I wasn't thinking about what church folk would say or think because I'm grown." "Yeah, you are grown but brother isn't and he almost got shot today because of you." "How"? I looked at my brother, waiting for his answer. "Well, I was playing basketball with some of the guys and a conversation got heated after I slapped one of the guys who started bragging. He didn't take my bragging too well and your name came up; actually, it was the comment that set me off." "What was the comment?" I asked? "He said to me that I needed to go and get my sister off the block and get you some help; that you were on crack. I walked up to him and said you're lying; my sister ain't on that stuff. All of the guys started to laugh so I looked at my best friend Deon and he shook his head and said, yeah man, it's true. They say she is always at the block buying and she lets Terry use her car for it. That's how we found you tonight." He got all teary eyed and left the room. I looked over at Vicky and she was in tears, sitting in the chair just looking at me, stunned. The big sister she looked up to had just let her down and in a big way. Her look was priceless. After all that was said, no more conversation for the night. We all went to bed. My mama stayed up for the rest of the night.

The next morning mama came in and woke me up and said "Come on, get up. Let's go to work." "Work! I don't feel like working." I felt like I needed to sleep for weeks. I got up anyway, got dressed and got in the car, ready for the questions. Since mom and I hadn't talked last night, I knew the questions were coming. Saturday's were always busy at our shop so this would help me with the craving I knew was bound to come. The ride there was filled with worship and praise music on CD, and no questions came from mama. We get to the shop and went to work just like it was a regular and normal day. My sister was still real quiet and teary eyed the whole day, still. I really felt bad that I had let her down, but I knew she and my family had already forgiven me. The day went by pretty fast. As we were cleaning up to leave for the day, my mama asked me, how? Why? "Mom, I am sorry; all I can tell you is that it just started after the hair show." Then my mom started naming off some friends' names of mine that I hung around with and told me and specifically "I want you to stay away from Ms. Pretty". I don't want you around her anymore." I told her *that* friendship had been severed and done with concerning that area. "Now, as to why, I really couldn't tell you why. It just happened and I enjoyed it. I enjoyed how it made me feel." "That's always been your problem girl; you have never been scared of anything." My sister shook her head. "Yep"! She finally asked, "Why didn't you come to me?" Shame was my answer. "I didn't want you to see all the flaws in my life. I always felt like a disappointment in some areas of my life; like I wasn't really myself inside, if you know what I mean. It's like I turned into someone else sometimes."

A few days went by and Sunday morning rolls in and it's time for church. Now we get ready for a one hour and a half trip to one of my dad's churches. Conversation of wow I already knew what this hour and a half was gonna be like. To my surprise, there were no questions from my father. We drive to church like we use to -- the norm -- when I was growing up. I helped him unload his things, gathered them all and went into both his office and the sanctuary to help get things ready. Then, church started. The members were very happy to see me; it seemed like hugs and kisses came from every direction. It felt great. All this time my little Tootie was still with my husband but I did see her yesterday at the shop. She did what she always does and that is: she runs up to me, and with a great big smile, says "Hi Mommy" and gives me the biggest hug ever. Her love for me was so unconditional. She had no clue what Mommy was doing; even on the nights I would wake her up and speed down the road for the drugs.

Anyway, first hymn starts and I look at my daddy and he looks so withdrawn and so very sad; he's full of tears; he can't stop crying. The tears just kept flowing. By the time the prayer comes around, I heard this loud moan and Jesus come behind that cry (plea). It was my mama; she had finally begun to release her tears. The whole church began to pray in the spirit. They knew something was hurting her but all they could do was pray. They knew it concerned me but they did not know what it was about or the specifics. They knew this because they had not seen me in years and then, all of a sudden, I show up looking like I weighed all but 100lbs. Actually, I am pretty sure some had an idea or figured out what it was. Daddy didn't really preach that day either. He just talked about praying for your children because the devil is always after them, but "I declare, on this day, he cannot and will not have mine", he said. So then the altar call was deliverance for me.

I vowed NEVER TO DO DRUGS again. I

rededicated my life back to the Lord that same evening because my father had called everyone up to the altar, and of course, I went up because I truly knew that I needed God right now, if I was gonna make it.

One week had passed and, so had I. I was passed from house to house. One grandma to the other would keep me, yes, keep me like a child trying to keep me from going back to the monster of a thing that had a grip on me. My uncle even came and picked me up one week and took me to every pawn shop I had been to, in an effort to get my jewelry back from every one of them, and I did too. This same uncle took me out of town for a week and called my husband to talk to him, in an effort to minister to him to support me. When we returned to our home town area, he, my husband, was waiting for me at my parents' house with papers in hand; no, not divorce papers, but for rehab. He said "I'm putting you in a facility where I'm stationed. This is the only way we can make this marriage work, that is, if you agree to go. Will you?" "Yeah", I said. You see, I realized that I needed to get away from being shifted from house to house. I needed my own house again. So now, a few days had passed as I gathered my belongings and my thoughts, to get ready for this journey or season of my life.

The ride to rehab was refreshing. My husband actually apologized for all the times he abused me by putting his hands on me, for all the affairs he was involved in and said that somewhere in this mess, he blamed himself for what I had done; all the while, I'm smiling from within, but still too afraid to smile on the outside. See, I heard his apologies before so I didn't trust that he wouldn't put his hands on me again if I made him mad. We pulled up to the facility and go in and oh no, the door locked behind me. I am in prison I thought to myself. I will be on a time schedule –theirs, of course. I definitely did not expect this. The very first day, I wanted to go home.

Now, the next day, I'm sitting on the edge of my assigned bed in my assigned room in rehab and the therapist comes in and asks me if I am coming to class? "What class" I asked. "They are new classes for our new people. It just tells you what to expect while you're here." "Okay", I told her. In laymen terms, it's orientation for new drug users. I'm sitting in this class and on comes a film on drug use and what it does to your mind and body. This film really took me to a place –a place that I had never saw or been before when I was on these drugs. The film informs you and reveals what your insides look like with the use of this drug –cocaine. Your insides are slowly but surely dying. It dries up your organs and darkens your teeth. Your teeth begin to turn black over time and your organs start to fail and/or shut down. Here I am smoking this stuff and I'm not even thinking about what it's doing to my body and my brain cells. Once your brain cells start dying, you don't get them back. I was at a loss for words. After an hour or so, more paperwork was passed out for us to read later and then I was scheduled to go to my therapy session after this so I just sat there and listened; I watched how the counselors facilitated the class, as they had other drug addicts discuss their lives and what they had done throughout their drug use.

Later that afternoon, I'm walking down the hall and

this girl comes up to me and speaks to me. I noticed that she was also in my class. She said she was wondering why I didn't raise my hand in class to ask questions. I told her "I didn't want to". She says, "Well it really would help". "How" I asked. "It's a release of things you weren't able to talk about to anyone else." "Like I said, I don't want to talk about it. I have my Bible. That's all I need." "Bible", she said. "Girl, they leave that in your drawer beside your bed." "No, not that Bible –my own Bible I brought from home." "Oh" was all she said and nothing else after that, except that she would see me at lunch.

I'm in counseling now with just my therapist and me. She starts off: "Let's begin; why don't you tell me how you got started and how long you have been an addict. I told her it was about six to eight months ago. Then, she made a quick expression, like she thought it was longer than that – like maybe years and not months. Anyway, I told her again that "Yes, it was six to eight months." She then asks, "You've done all of this financial abuse in that period of time?" I said yes. She asked me if I had sold anything out of my house or sold myself for it. "Absolutely not" I told her. "I would never do that." She looked at me and said very firmly, that "Eventually you would have, believe me; you would have." I just looked at her and said "No, I wouldn't have." She said "Trust me, you would have." Right then, I made up in my mind at that time that I would not be going back to counseling. I KNEW all I needed to do was stay in my room with both the Word of God and the Lord Himself; I didn't even go to the cafeteria to eat that day. I fasted, prayed and read my Word. At that very moment in my life, I knew I had to get to Jesus for myself.

A week went by and I called my husband and told him I was ready to come home. He asked me did I really think things had changed that much in a week. I said "Yes they have and I'm now ready to come home. He said "What if I told you I got orders out of the country. "What, where?" "Germany", he tells me. Then I tell him that "I think it will be good for us to get away." I wasn't even thinking about him hitting me; I just knew I needed to get away from where I was right now; it wasn't good for me anymore. There were too many familiar spirits.

The next day my husband did come to pick me up and we stayed with my parents. Shortly that day, he left way ahead of us to get housing ready for us. This left me home with my parents for little over three months. For days and weeks I remember saying to myself *oh please hurry up man*. When he would call to check in, my conversations were mostly asking him to please hurry things up. "It's coming girl; just be patient." Actually we needed this time apart also. I was really, I mean really missing him, and according to him, he was missing me too.

Mama, of course, planned a celebration/going away hair show which was by the way sold out. It was probably due to the nosy people in my hometown who wanted to see how I was really doing after the drug stint. Of course it was amazing and also very tearful. All of my clients, all of her clients, friends and family were crying because I was leaving. It was the best hair show by far we ever had.

The next couple of days I was saying my goodbyes to neighbors and getting myself ready for my departure. Driving to the airport, my father looked at me in the mirror and said "You've done well; enjoy yourself in Germany and stay in church. Don't forget your foundation; it's always gonna be God. Keep Him first and you'll be okay." At this time you could walk the person to their gate at the airport. We cried and prayed, prayed and cried until they called our assigned seat numbers. My child and I boarded the plane with snot and tears running down our faces. I couldn't even look back; I knew my mama was a mess. Our flight was long; it was actually my first time on a plane. We ate; we slept; and we watched movies and did the same things all over again during the entire flight. The flight seemed like it was almost 24 hours long. When we arrived in Frankfurt, Germany, I was in awe to be in another country and this was a beautiful country. My husband was there at the arriving gate area to receive us. He had purchased a van a few weeks before. It was actually a nice van, but when we pulled up to the military housing, I was less than happy. First, of all it was apartment looking. I said to him, "These don't look like what I saw on the Internet." "I know", he said. These are the new sections of the military housing; what we looked at on the Internet were the old ones and the old ones are for the officers. "Oh, okay" I said. "Where are the washing and dryer machines then", I asked, because I didn't see them. "Oh, they are in the basement girl along with extra storage closets. We will be okay." "I know we will be okay because I ain't lugging nothing up these steps. I'm not lugging no laundry baskets, no groceries – nothing." He just smiled and so did I because I knew I would be doing just the opposite.

Settling in now and I'm bored. So now it's been a couple of weeks and I am so bored in an unfamiliar territory. I have no job, no friends; just doing wife and mother duties. Smiley comes home and says we have a guest coming over to talk about investing. *Oh man, another get rich scheme* I'm thinking in my head.

"Investments"

So the guy comes over and sits down, pulls out all of this paperwork. Initially, from what I could see, it was legitimate paperwork. It actually was investing (money market, stocks, etc.) and he actually was quite good at what he discussed and shared with us. He was also quite handsome. Aww man, we had to cross eyes at this meeting a time or two. A knock at the door the following day took me by surprise. I'm thinking its hubby so I have on my shorts and tank top, thinking that he forgot his key or something. I open the door. Here is this investment guy in a suit, tie, looking oh so nice and here I am half naked standing in front of him at the door. "Wow!" he said and continued. "Hi. I just wanted to stop by and bring you guys the rest of the information I promised you and to let you know I'm in the next building over if you have any questions." I take the paperwork and brochures and turn to put them on the counter and look back to tell him thank you and he looks like the fox on the cartoons with his eyes bulging out of his head and with his tongue lying on the floor. I smirk at him and tell him thanks again. He says "You're very welcome my beautiful neighbor." I close the door and go to the window to see which building he goes in. About 15 minutes later I hear keys in the door and it is Smiley. He notices the paperwork on the counter and asked where it came from. I said "The guy just dropped them off. "Did you let him in here dressed like that?" "No" I said. "He handed them to me at the door. It wasn't a lie; he did. "Okay" he said. "I don't want any men in my house while I'm gone." "Okay dear." I had to get out of this house; it was driving me crazy. I always had a job because I started working at 16. Well, at least he had finally brought me a little car. I'm dressed to go out, looking for a job, where I saw a sign "Hairstylist Wanted", which of course is my forte --my area of expertise.

I had called the salon where I saw the wanted sign and spoke with the owner on the phone. We scheduled a day for me to come in for an interview, so, on this particular day, I get into my little car and it won't start up. Thinking for a few minutes, crazy me, I realized that I had left the lights on and didn't know it. I open the hood and bend over as if I knew what I was looking for and also thinking that I should try to get a jump from someone. Guess who comes over to help with a big grin on his face. "Wow! You look nice today. "Thanks" I said. "I have a job interview near the PX (Post Exchange). Guess I had better start walking."

"Oh, no you won't. I'll take you." "Oh no, you trying to get me beat up or what!" "Beat up – no; I'm trying to help you and if he's beating you, you need to leave. You're too pretty and fine for that." Stroking my ego was what he was doing and he knew it. He appeared to be a mature business man who was polished and refined and I liked what I saw.

He suggested he drop me off and I can walk back to make it look good in case Smiley came home. "Okay", I said. So, he dropped me off at the PX and asked me to have lunch with him. I said maybe because it depends on if I get this job or not. Well, I did my thing and showed them my stuff and I got the job. Yeah, out of this house and got my own money now. The next day Smiley put a new battery in my car and I was good to go. From time to time, I would see Mr. Investor passing and I would wave. Lately, I noticed him and Mr. Smiley were talking more and more also. One day, we receive an unexpected visit from him again. A knock on the door one evening and it is Mr. Investor and his family, including his wife, who wanted to come over and welcome us to the community, as well as to ask where the salon shop was, so that she could start getting her hair done. She shared with me, from what she was told, that there were no good beauticians over there and told me that I was a definite welcome for some ailing heads. I'm gonna tell everyone I know about you, she said. "Thanks" I said and then I asked her what she did. She said that she was a sergeant which is how they got military housing because Mr. Investor was not in the military. "Oh, I see; I was just wondering" I said. Then Mr. Investor said "We have to get you guys to come over for dinner next week. I looked at Smiley and he answered "Okay man." Mr. Investor and I caught each other's eye and smiled. There was clearly a mutual attraction taking place here.

So now, it's time to head over to our newfound neighbors for dinner. Fourth floor and here I thought our third floor was bad, but we made it. Both our daughter, Tootie and their kids took off to his son's room to play and watch TV. So here we all are now, sitting at their kitchen table drinking wine and having appetizers. Shrimp scampi was one of the appetizers. I couldn't leave them alone. I told her I needed her recipe for this. Her reply was "Oh, Vestie made that dish." Hmm, smart, handsome and can cook; I need to stay away from this man.

By this time, all Ten Commandments had been broken by me and if there was a 11th commandment, that commandment would have been broken by me too.

Dinner was great and so was the conversation. We all agreed that we would do this get together thing more often. "Sure" Smiley said "no problem. The next meal is at our house." I couldn't get my mind off of this man so I waited for Smiley to go to work the next day and made sure she was gone and I went and knocked on the door. This man comes to the door with nothing on but a towel and he is dripping wet. I clear my throat and say are you busy. He looks down at himself and says not yet and the towel begins to move. I try not to look because I know where this could lead. "Would you please put some clothes on?" "No, he said, what's up". I asked him was I crazy or was I imagining things, or was he trying to start something here. The towel has a full rise now and his reply to me was to look down. "Does that answer your question beautiful lady?" "Yeah, it does, so I need to let you know that my husband is crazy and I don't think we should start anything. I am not trying to lose my clients nor your wife as my only friend here in this foreign place." "Understood", he said and I turned to walk away. He said "See you later". I turned back to say "Okay" and his towel was completely off now because he was drying off the rest of his body and asked me what I had on under my dress. I laughed and said "Nothing; I frequently wear nothing because I don't like to sweat." "Um, um, um "he said as he closed the door.

I won't lie. I was intrigued by this man. Maybe it's

because he was just that – a man and not these boys I had dealt with in my young adult life.

I worked today as usual and later in the morning, a beautiful bouquet of flowers is delivered to me. Wow! The card reads "Just a taste of you is all I'm looking for." I knew who they were from. I left them on my station. I get home, I cook a nice dinner and later, I made sweet passionate love to my husband, just as if it was him who sent me the flowers. Well, it wasn't like wam, bam and thank you ma'am; it was my husband and somehow I knew where this would lead to if I didn't stay away from this other man, Mr. Investor, so I think again.

As usual, 6 am Saturday morning and Smiley is up and out, but at least he had washed my car, just as he usually does. I would see him closer to dusk on Saturday, always had some excuse to go somewhere on Saturdays. My baby girl was outside playing as usual and I noticed Vestie's wife was gone too. I shook my head and loaded up the laundry basket and headed to the laundry room which was shared by the units on my side. I'm putting the clothes in the dryer, listening to my little cassette player with my headphones and I feel a hand up the back of my dress that went to the right spot. I turned around and he says as I take my ear plugs out. "Wow!" Nothing under there was the truth, huh!" He was washing their clothes, now, what an untimely coincidence, or should I say a timely coincidence. I finished putting my clothes in the washer and listening to my music. He comes back and asks me to help him put some old mattresses in their closet that he had drug downstairs. I carried one end and he picked up the other end. He opened the door and I went in first. What was I thinking? He had to close the door behind us to get the mattresses in the corner, which he did. He put them in the corner on the floor. I went around the mattress and around him to open the door but his hand went up my dress again and his arm around my neck. His breath was on the back of my neck. I tried to resist. This spirit was too much for me so I gave in to temptation –again. A taste is what he got because that's all he wanted, at that point.

The closet became our secret spot on Saturdays and Mondays and his office became an additional spot on Tuesdays, Wednesdays and Thursdays if I could get away. A serious affair was in the making. We could not stay away from each other. We would have lunch every day and have our secret *rendezvous* when we could get away.

One very pleasant day I am here at work, chilling. We were not too busy so we were just sitting around talking in the shop and in walks this guy who I thought was from Jamaica because of his dreads and his accent. He asked if he could use the phone and of course we said yes. His call was short. Then he turned to say thank you and then he asked me, after I said you're welcome, if I sing. "Yeah, I sing a little" I said. So he says, "I'm in the studio next door. Come on over when you get a chance. I wanna record you." "Oh, ok" I said. I did not get the chance to go over to the studio this same week so the next week he was back asking me again to come over. A break came for me so I went over to see what this guy wanted me to sing. He had two females and one guy in there with him. The guy was German; a

Czechoslovakian female, and the other female, who my eyes were immediately drawn to, was very pretty -- half German and half black. Serena was her name. We became friends right away.

We all sat and talked and fiddled around in the studio, singing to different tracks which he was about to replay. When he did, I was in shock at what he had done with us just playing around. "CoCo (he had given me a nickname) I need you to lay some tracks and background for me. I'll pay you good. I also need you to help these girls. I'm putting them in a group and I need you to be their vocal mentor, as well as their hairstylist. We are getting ready to do a music video for our new single on the charts, 'Dancing with Tears in my Eyes'." "Oh, wow". What a great opportunity this was for me; I was all in. So excited, I went home and told my husband. He wasn't happy at all. He shrugged at the idea, immediately. He was not on board with it at all. I told Vestie and he was even more excited than I was. I'm so proud of you he kept saying.

With tour dates set, video rehearsals several days a week and hair appointments constantly, gee, we are rolling now. Oh gee, here we come, Spain, Austria, Czechoslovakia, Italy, Paris, Switzerland, oops, sorry, that was with Mr. Investor on ski trips every two to three months it seemed like. We had fallen for each other hard. Fallen in love actually, and we made plans to leave our spouses, get married and live happily ever after. I was never home. If I wasn't doing hair for the tour, I was with Vestie on a trip somewhere. He wined and dined me. Well, almost a year into the relationship with him, we both became careless and some of my personals that I had given him, his wife found in his desk drawer at their home, along with cards, letters that he was supposed to throw away after reading (which he had not). She had proof of us now and it was about to hit the fan.

I had to go and apologize to this woman for falling in love with her husband and beg her to not tell mine. I knew he would kill me. We promised that we would stop seeing each other in order for her not to tell Mr. Smiley. Ask me -

-did we? Of course not! We just slowed down a bit and with me being on tour, this also helped. He was able to get away and being that I was out singing, I was already available to meet up with him. Still, we couldn't get enough of each other. He would lie as to where he was going. His scheduled conferences and his business meetings picked up so he also had a great front.

A lie is what it was. I completely thought this man and I would marry each other. Oh yes, a lying trick of the enemy, yet again. We loved each other so much that his wife knew we were still messing around and she put in orders for another base. Yep, he told me while we were in Austria on a ski trip that he was leaving and that he would send for me when he got settled. I continued with my singing career until we didn't get paid for our first single. Great success in Europe but no Euros in my hand ended it for me. My mama always told me, nothing in life is free.

Well, my singing career ended and I'm back at home doing what I loved to do, working and having my clients satisfied with their hair. However, my clientele was not where it had been when I started singing. I lost a few and some of my faithful ones hung in there with me. Of the few that hung in with me, there were two at my house under the dryers when Mr. Smiley came home one day in one of his moods. He came in the kitchen and asked if he could speak with me. My response was when I'm done with my clients I will talk to you. I could already see the look on his face and I knew his day wasn't good so my night wouldn't be either. Before I could turn back around to get me a drink out of the refrigerator, I'm in a choke held position being drug to my bedroom by this crazy man. My clients immediately jumped up to tell him to stop and they also tried to stop him from dragging me into the bedroom. I've never seen anything like it in my life. He picks both of them up and throws them into the back of the couch, flipping the couch over and almost into the glass coffee table. He then proceeds to drag me to the bedroom. My clients run out and begin banging on my neighbor's door for her to call Military Police. We get to the door of the bedroom and there is my daughter, dripping wet and naked as a jay bird (as my mom would say) standing in the bathroom door, where she was taking a bath, saying "Daddy, daddy, you said you weren't gonna hit Mommy anymore." The look on her face was priceless and I turned around and grabbed the vase off of the coffee table and clocked this man upside the head as hard as I could. It felt great; it was the first time I fought him back like that and it felt great. He actually let me go. By this time Military Police came, got statements from the both of us, as well as my clients. But guess what, they arrested me too. What, you asked. "Yeah, I'm baffled too, but they arrest me because I also hit him. I couldn't believe they were arresting me too. We get to the MP station and re-tell our statement again there. My husband dropped the charges filed against me and I kept the charges I filed against him. He got anger management classes, again and I did get a restraining order, again. He was not supposed to come around the complex for six months until he finished his anger management classes. I was to go to spousal abuse classes to understand the pressure military men are under and talk to his captain which I did and it led to nowhere. We also had to do couples' counseling for six months.

However by the third month I knew this was getting us nowhere too. He couldn't even admit that he had a problem, but then the sixth month rolled around and he was back at home a changed man, so he said. Somewhere within the last three months of his counseling the light came on, so I took advantage of the light coming on too. I called Mr. Investor whose wife had received orders to report to Arizona (which they did relocate there) and told him what had happened. In the meanwhile, Mr. Investor and I had made plans for me to leave Smiley and come there. But first, I had to convince Mr. Smiley that I needed a vacation before I came to Arizona. I told him that I needed to go and see my mama for a few weeks and I would be back. Of course, Mr. Smiley paid for it. He felt guilty as usual. My plans were to go see my mama for a week and Mr. Investor for the other week.

I packed a few bags and I am now on my way to Frankfurt Airport, still planning in my head how this was gonna work out. I'm standing there waiting to show my passport and go through Customs, all the while shaking in my shoes. Finally I get through Customs. I look back at him, smile and give him the peace sign. Yep, I made it. I was finally done with this man out of my life, and he was, for now. His look was priceless. My heart was still not at peace though; notice I said I gave him the peace sign. I had to leave my baby girl to get away from this man. I knew he would figure it out if I asked him if I could take her. The worse day of my life by far was the day I left my baby, but I knew I would see her soon.

By the time I got back to the States and to my mama's house, my daddy said that boy has called here at least fifty times. What have you done girl. I sat down with both of my parents and told them how many years this man had abused me; nine in total. My mom waited for the phone to ring again and it did. She told him you better send me my grand baby ASAP. He said she left her; what makes you think I'm gonna send her now. He knew what my mama was like and she meant every word she said. You better know he knew immediately after that statement because all he said was "yes ma'am". She didn't play and he knew it.

His career would be over in the blink of an eye by the time she hung up the phone with his captain.

I never made it to Arizona. I saw no need. It was December 1999 when I left this man. I got my daughter back June 15, 2000, three days after school was out. We were now safe and happy.

One day I was talking to my parents and my father asked "Why would you not give him another chance?" I gave him a double-take look and said "Daddy, are you serious!" He said "Yes I am. I'm sure it couldn't have been all that bad. You know you have a mouth on you just like your mama." "Yes, I do" I said, "But in all the years that I've known you and mama daddy, I have never seen you put your hands on her." His look was all so priceless! After that, I made plans to move out to California, so now I was saying goodbye. I needed to begin a new life on a good note for both me and my baby...

...and with that "goodbye" a second book would be birthed.

CPSIA information can be obtained
at www.ICGtesting.com
Printed in the USA
FFOW04n1653140116
20448FF